GREAT WHITE HOUSE 2: Billary Bites Back

by

Christoph Paul
&
Arthur Graham

ISBN: 978-1-944866-03-7

Published by Clash Books
Cover by Justin T. Coons

Index

EMERGENCY. RED LEVEL EMERGENCY.

Twelve hours ago, Washington, D.C. was flooded by weather-modulated storms and infiltrated by genetically modified sharks.

All naval bases were hit by these storms, and the terrorist sharks are still at large.

We regret to inform you that the President, Vice President, and leaders of the House and Senate have all perished. We are actively seeking government officials to refill these crucial roles.

We are now working with the armed forces, the NSA, and other government agencies in our efforts to gather more information.

There is grave concern that these coordinated storm/shark attacks are only just the beginning of something much larger and global in scale.

ACT 1

Chapter 1

NSA Headquarters: Washington, D.C.

The nation may have been under attack, but besides that, it was really just another day at the NSA. Seated in row upon row of cubicles, government employees were busily monitoring our latest tweets, texts, sexts, Instagram pics, iCloud uploads, Kindle purchases, and Facebook posts. These were people who were not quite smart enough to get into the CIA, but loved watching all five seasons of *Homeland*.

They were not all that brave or heroic, this much was true, but they honestly believed they were making America a safer place. Through surveillance. Before joining the NSA, they were unemployed Americans spending the majority of their time patrolling social media, arguing over the legitimacy of the latest memes, and admiring leaked nude celebrity photos.

They had finally found a job that suited their particular skill set.

In fact, about the only person who didn't love working for the NSA was its Director, Admiral Michael S. Rodgers. He hadn't been appointed all that long ago, but already he'd grown sick of babysitting hackers, nerds, and perverts day in and day out. He missed the open sea and working directly with the military, doing meaningful work for his country.

Today, though, there was a real crisis happening in D.C. The entire city had been flooded, and sharks had invaded the White House and its environs overnight. Admiral Rodgers wanted desperately to help, but here he was trapped at NSA headquarters instead. Due to flooding in the area, he'd been sequestered there since yesterday along with his entire staff.

The chain of command had ordered him to stay put and dig up intel on the attacks. Of course, Admiral Rodgers thought that this was a total waste of time. This was nature happening out there, not terrorism. There would not be any tweets, emails, or text messages that would show them how to stop things like bad weather and hungry sharks. Maybe you could negotiate with terrorists, but not with forces of nature.

Back in his younger days, when he was stationed in the Pacific, the Admiral had witnessed the brutality of these creatures up close. While out on a routine diving exercise with his friend, Private Thompson, a great white shark had appeared out of nowhere. Somehow Rodgers was able to get out of the way in time, but Thompson hadn't been so lucky. The shark ripped off the private's right arm and a full third of his torso with one savage bite. Eyes wild with fear and pain, the doomed sailor sunk out of sight, never to return from the ocean floor.

To this day, the Admiral still had nightmares about losing his friend in such a horrific manner.

They had been cooped up at NSA headquarters since yesterday, prevented from leaving due to flooding in the area. Earlier that morning, the emergency notification had informed them that the President was dead, and that all citizens remaining in the D.C. area were in grave danger.

Being a lifelong Navy man, Admiral Rodgers obeyed his orders, but he wished he were out there doing something useful, like leading a fleet against the sharks instead.

The only good thing about their office was that it was well protected from threats like storms and sharks. Hidden in the southeast ghettos of D.C., the building had no windows and was built from steel. He'd never heard of a shark capable of biting through steel before, bioengineered or not, but this did little to remedy his cabin fever.

This sense of being trapped and powerless had him feeling anxious and on-edge. He paced in circles around the office, doing his best to ignore the despised workers at their computer terminals. The NSA headquarters looked more like a goddamned telemarketing center or a library for special needs children than any government surveillance installation, he thought.

Stopping by the desk of one of his least-favorite workers, Thomas Crowntree, Rodgers wasn't at all surprised to find the prick openly displaying pornography on his computer.

"Anything productive, Crowntree?" Admiral Rodgers asked, pretending to ignore all the ass-pounding, ball-slapping action. "Find any info on the attacks?"

Crowntree was twenty-five, a senator's son, and a real pain in the ass. No one knew this but Rodgers and himself, but Crowntree had been the hacker responsible for the infamous Fappening leak. And, of course, Rodgers had to protect the little weasel because of who his father was.

"Well?"

Crowntree just laughed and said, "Seriously Admiral, I thought you wanted us to *avoid* indulging in these crazy conspiracy theories. Shitty weather and shark attacks. What can you do?"

"Your *job* is what," Rodgers replied. "Just what in the hell have you been doing since we've been cooped up here, anyway?"

"Well, I've found nothing on sharks or terrorists so far, but I *did* manage to uncover some new nudes of Taylor Swift. I should really share them around the office, you know? Could be good for morale."

"Jesus..." Admiral Rodgers said and shook his head.

Hours passed and the rain stayed heavy.

This storm was unlike anything Rogers had ever experienced. Even back when he'd been stationed in the tropics of East Asia as a lowly deckhand, never had he encountered a monsoon of such force.

Earlier that morning, when the storm had abruptly stopped for a brief period, Rodgers felt a sudden sense of elation, but it was squashed when the rain began falling just as heavily as before. Scientifically, it seemed as though the eye of the storm had passed over them, but in Rodgers' mind it was more like some asshole had pressed a magic button to resume the storm.

Just to piss him off.

The Admiral had been through enough storms to know that this weather wasn't natural. It almost felt like God was telling the Capital that He or She or whatever you call It was dissatisfied with all of America, but Rodgers was not what you would call a superstitious man.

Putting the thought out of his head, he was debating going back to his office for another shot of Jack when Eddie Little called him over.

Eddie 'Tea Time" Little was an ex-hacker and one of

Rodger's best employees. The kid looked like a freak with all his tattoos and the multiple holes in his ears and face, but he did good work and was always the smartest one in the room.

Rodgers never called him "Tea Time" personally, but he had liked Little from the start. He remembered visiting the half Black, half Asian kid in prison a few years ago. Little was facing a heavy sentence for hacking into Match.com and making himself a perfect match for every attractive girl between the ages of 18 and 25. The Admiral explained to Little that he could get him out of prison if he agreed to work for the NSA.

The kid looked disheveled and beat up, sitting there in his orange jumpsuit, and the Admiral knew he wouldn't last long behind bars. Little decided to accept the plea bargain after less than two minutes of conversation.

"What is it, Little?" Admiral Rodgers asked him. "Tell me you've got something good?"

Tea Time usually maintained a cool and collected appearance around the office, but now his olive brown skin seemed a few shades paler. He didn't even look up at Rodgers as the Admiral walked over to his workstation.

His eyes remained locked on his monitor, his mouth hanging open in awe at what he saw.

On the screen was a jumble of encrypted text, chunks of data that Little had been mining all morning. He had deciphered it and procured valuable intel on the origin of the sharks, a mole in the NSA, and rumors of a secret island where things much worse than just biologically enhanced sharks were possibly being made.

He flipped his asymmetrical bangs over his left eye as Rodgers approached. "Sir," he said in a hushed tone, still staring at his screen, "I think we should discuss this in your office."

"Okay son," Rodgers said, "follow me."

Crowntree overheard them. He continued to focus on Taylor Swift's naked pics while the men walked away. Waiting until the Admiral's office door closed behind them, he got up and slid over to Tea Time's workstation.

In all actuality, Crowntree couldn't care less about naked women; he was gay and a genius as well. So smart that he'd even mastered the art of looking like an incompetent pervert, just some rich kid reaping the benefits of nepotism, but even his powerfully connected father had no idea that Thomas Crowntree was working for someone besides the NSA.

Typing in Tea Time's password, Crowntree smiled as he read through the decrypted text. *Yes*, he thought to himself, *all is going according to plan. I must notify The Don at once.*

Using an untraceable email address, he began composing the following message: Things are going well, but I'm afraid the NSA might finally be onto us. You'll repay me when all is said and done, sparing my life as promised? TC.

Crowntree hit Send and imagined that special day, fantasizing about the hedonistic party The Don was sure to throw for him on his own private island. Through his loyal service, he was certain he'd be accepted as one of the elect.

He pictured all the underwear model slaves, snorting coke off their big hard dicks, feeling his own (albeit much smaller) dick growing hard as well. He was just about to excuse himself to the bathroom for a little relief when something slammed against the exterior wall of the NSA headquarters, shaking the whole entire building.

SLAM!!!

SLAM, SLAM!!!

Workers began to scream as the wall dented inward.

A baby megalodon blasted through the wall.

"NOOOO!!!" Crowntree screamed as his bowels involuntarily voided themselves. "I was *supposed* to be spared!"

It was larger than an adult great white and twice as ravenous.

Crowntree spun around and dove over Tea Time's desk. The baby megalodon lunged at him and snatched his legs in midair. Like a garbage disposal grinding down on a pile of chicken wings, its jaws reduced him to bone paste.

The other NSAers fled for the exits, screaming their prayers to God or the higher power of their choosing, as if He/She/It could save them from the megalodon menace.

Another baby megalodon burst through the wall, this time closer to the floor, heralding a flood of rushing water. Then another, and another. Soon the terrified workers were waist deep in water, with sharks surrounding them from all sides.

A few of the NSAers near the Admiral's office tried to escape within, but the water pressure prevented them from prying open its door.

"PLEASE, GOD!!!"

"AAAHHHHHHHHH!!!"

"NOOOOOOOOOOOOOOOOO!!!"

There was simply nowhere left to go but down into the bellies of the giant baby megalodons. Their entire office became a blood bath of shredded emails and human flesh.

Just as Tea Time finished telling Admiral Rodgers the dire intel he'd uncovered, that was when the first shark attacked. Though the retired Navy SEAL had been stunned by the news, he was quickly slapped out of it by the sounds of screaming and carnage just outside his door.

"Shit!" he cursed, unable to believe it.

"How is this even possible?" Tea Time asked. "What the fucking fuck?!"

"It's like somehow they *knew* to send the sharks here..." Rodgers replied.

"Great, that's just fucking great. *Psychic* giant sharks? We are so fucking dead."

"Shhhhh! Be *quiet*...."

Something long and large bumped against the office door then, slowly scraping past it. Water had begun to seep into the room.

"Listen, Little," Rodgers whispered, "we need to leak this intel of yours to *everyone*, before it's—"

They'd noticed the screams had stopped.

"We're next," Tea Time whispered, an audible tremor in his

voice.

"We may not have much time," Rodgers replied. "Quick, do it now!"

Tea Time scrambled over to the other side of his desk, attempting to operate the computer.

When the next megalodon bumped against the door, it was harder, more purposeful this time. Rodgers saw that a crack had formed in its sturdy wooden frame and slowly backed away.

"Did you get it through, Little? Please, tell me you got it through."

"It won't send..." he whimpered in response. "These sharks, they killed our fucking towers, and now they're gonna kill us...."

"Screw *us*, Little," Rodgers said. "We don't matter, if what you told me is true. This is not just national security on the line here—this is *global* security we're talking about!"

Unable to hold them back any longer, a torrent of tears came streaming down Tea Time's face. "I don't wanna die," he sobbed. "I'm so fucking scared, Sir...."

"Get ahold of yourself, Little!"

The Admiral rarely got scared, but it was not himself he was worried about. He knew that he wouldn't be able to stop these sharks or even save his own ass, but if they could just get this intel to the right people, they might at least give the world a chance.

SLAM!!!

Rodgers and Tea Time tumbled backwards as the megalodon rammed the office wall, its teeth tearing a hole in the door. Through this opening appeared one black, beady eye, searching for prey. The Admiral saw nothing but hunger and death in that eye, and he knew they'd need nothing short of a miracle if they expected to survive.

If he was going to die, he didn't want himself or Tea Time to die in those jagged jaws.

Going for the gun he kept in his desk drawer, Rodgers turned to Tea Time and chambered a round. "I'll make this quick and painless for you. May God have mercy on our souls!"

Accepting his fate, Tea Time forced himself to put his hands together, praying to the God his African-American father taught him to believe in as a child.

Our Father, who art in heaven, hallowed be thy—

BOOM!!!

"Get on the boat, now!"

Tea Time and Admiral Rodgers wiped the dust from their faces and stared at the massive hole in the back wall of his office.

"We don't have much time!" a familiar female voice called out to them from somewhere up on deck. "Hurry, climb aboard, but don't touch the trident—it's still hot! That is an *order* from your president!"

The bow of the yacht was sticking right through the office wall. Mounted upon it was a golden trident held by a marble statue of Poseidon. Each of its three prongs still crackled with residual electricity, which packed enough charge to melt through steel.

"Well?! What are you two idiots waiting for?"

Tea Time and Rodgers climbed aboard as ordered, and were greeted by a sight even weirder than the one they'd just witnessed.

"Gaddafi!" barked the same woman, still obscure in the early dawn light. "Have your girls prepare to open fire."

It was then the Admiral finally recognized her. While it was kind of hard to tell beneath the gaudy swashbuckler get-up, he saw that it was none other than President Hillary Clinton.

Joining her on deck were former Secretary of State, Condoleezza Rice, and former ruler of Libya, Muammar Gaddafi. Beside the reportedly deceased dictator stood a small cadre of bikinied, black-veiled mercenaries, each of them armed with an assortment of bladed weapons and automatic rifles.

Standing behind them was Hillary's husband and America's forty-first president, Bill Clinton. Lounging in a white windbreaker that looked more like a smoking jacket on him, he gave the Admiral and Tea Time an amiable thumbs up from afar.

Standing there beside Bill was another older white man whom Roberts immediately recognized as Jeffrey Epstein, American financier and registered sex-offender. He had once been convicted for activities involving underage girls on this very same yacht, which he had christened the *Jailbaiter*.

Bill nudged Epstein and said, "I love it when Gaddafi's girls fire those big ol' guns. All that recoil make their boobies bounce just right. Bikini girls and machine guns, that's the good stuff, bud."

Epstein just shrugged and said, "Eh, they're a bit too old for me...."

Meanwhile, Gaddafi had ordered them into attack formation.

"Ready..." he began.

Roberts and Tea Time froze, staring down the barrels of half a dozen AK-47s.

"Aim..."

The Admiral grabbed Tea Time and they both hit the deck.

"Fire!"

Gaddafi's Amazonian Guard opened fire on the baby megalodons in the office behind them, raining burning hot shell casings down upon their heads. The bikinied battle wenches laid waste to the bioengineered monstrosities with salvo after salvo of precision bursts of fire. Several of the sharks swam-charged the yacht, only to be mowed down before they'd even made it on deck.

When the smoke began to clear, there was nothing left but bloody shark carcasses piled up in the Admiral's former office.

Bill Clinton gave another enthusiastic thumbs up. "I love it when they do that!" he said. "It makes me feel so optimistic, and a little hard."

"Shut up, Bill!" Hillary ordered, looking extra imposing in her velvet tricorn hat. A long, black feather gave it an added touch of panache.

"Alright buttercup," Bill said, smiling and nodding in acquiescence. "That's my baby, so proud!"

Hillary just shook her head in annoyance and refocused her

attention on Tea Time and Admiral Rodgers.

"Men," she ordered, "come with me to the helm."

Knowing better than to question a direct order from their Commander in Chief, they followed President Clinton to the captain's wheel without delay.

"Admiral," she said, taking the wheel, "I'll have you man the ship, but first I'll hear your report. Salute the President when she addresses you, keeping rank and command."

"Yes, Ma'am!" Rodgers said, saluting her with pride. Despite everything that had happened, he was glad to see that America was still functioning as a nation.

"Good to have you aboard, Admiral. Now, please bring me up to date. What have you been able to learn about these sharks?"

"Yes, Madam President," Rodgers began. "I'm afraid that credit goes to my associate here, Edward Little."

Tea Time saluted the president as well.

"This shark situation," the Admiral continued, "bad as it may be, this is *nothing* compared to what's coming on the horizon!"

"What on earth could you possibly mean?"

Hillary went back to steering the ship, and Tea Time finally spoke up. "What the Admiral says is true, Madam President," he said. "These sharks here in D.C. are scary as shit, but based on what we've learned, they're going to be the least of our concerns."

"Admiral, will you and your associate please get to the fucking point?"

"I apologize, Madam President," Rodgers replied, "but Mr. Little here has uncovered a plot that is not just a threat to America, but to the whole entire worl—"

His report was interrupted by a massive splash, followed by an ominous shadow that fell across the deck. Rearing up over the starboard side of the *Jailbaiter* was none other than the mother megalodon herself, eyes glowing red with hate.

Spreading her pectoral fins, she was even wider than the yacht. Though fairly well tattered by this point, the glorious Chinese flag still adorned her dorsal fin.

Before Gaddafi's guards could fire a single shot, she descended upon them with all the fury of bereavement, devouring all six scantily-clad women in one ferocious bite.

"Madam President, we *must* survive this!" the Admiral cried. "We must inform the world of the ISIS plot, and their Sharks of Singularity!"

Chapter 2

The Great Mosque: Mecca, Saudi Arabia

No matter how long John Cardinal had been undercover as a Muslim for the CIA, he could never get used to having a beard. It always felt so alien to him, a constant reminder that he was living a lie, but as he looked upon the Ka'ba along with his Islamic brothers, he felt the tears of truth roll down into that tangled mass of hair on his face.

The CIA had prepared him for the many pitfalls that came with posing as a devout Muslim, but the one they didn't prepare him for was the possibility of actually embracing the faith.

Agent Cardinal looked at the men who were considered his prime targets, but for this moment they were only fellow Muslims shedding tears of joy before the holy Ka'ba. These were men who'd spent countless hours bonding over their hatred for the West, but their hatred for anyone and anything was completely subdued before the biggest, holiest cube in all of Islam.

The Ka'ba was believed to have been built by Abraham and Ishmael, and it was said that all those who underwent the pilgrimage to it would feel true reverence for the monotheistic faiths—the People of the Book.

Only now did Agent Cardinal and his friends understand what that term meant. They had traveled far from Muenster to Medina to Mecca, and now that they'd finally arrived, they felt a connection much bigger than themselves expressed in the names of God, Allah, and Yahweh.

Cardinal, who went by the alias Ibrahim, felt that the Ka'ba had the eyes of Allah. And while his friends basked in their loving gaze, all they did was make him remember his falsehood.

He remembered approaching his friends for the first time at the German mosque. He'd said he was a devout American Muslim who'd left his country due to its growing Islamophobia to study abroad.

They'd bonded over their shared feelings of alienation in the West and went out for some halal gyros afterwards. Weeks later, they all became flatmates, and soon John Cardinal found that he was no longer just playing the role of a young American Muslim, he was becoming one for real.

His superiors in the CIA had told him that these players were a sleeper cell on the rise, but after sharing all the highs and lows that came with several years of friendship, he saw that they were really just young men like himself, just trying to make some sense of an age that made little sense to them.

Cardinal, a secular man who'd grown up without any faith, was finding great beauty in Islam, a purpose to his life he never really knew he needed. When he'd first begun praying in mosques, it had just been for show, but it wasn't long before he'd forged a genuine relationship with Allah.

Eventually he stopped reporting to the CIA and agreed to go on the pilgrimage to Mecca without even taking official leave. He chose to serve Allah over America and felt peace he had never known before.

There before the Ka'ba, he did his best to forget who he really was, but there was just no continuing his lie under the watchful eyes of Allah. He wouldn't just be lying to himself or his friends anymore; he'd be lying to God.

The other truth he knew in his heart was that these men were not terrorists. They may have hated the West and all its materialistic culture, but they did not seek to bring harm to it.

They'd simply been alienated by a people who feared and didn't accept them. Governments that would bomb any nation with an Arabic-sounding name. They felt like outsiders in their own countries, but there in front of the Ka'ba, all were recognized as God's children.

He understood that this lie was the only thing keeping him from being a true Muslim. He felt that if he could finally let it go, he could finally be at one with the truth and the love of Allah. He'd be forgiven by his brothers, he knew, if only he could muster the courage to tell them.

"My brothers," Agent Cardinal said in Arabic to his friends, still crying tears of joy. "I cannot keep the lies hidden in my heart any longer. Please come close before we pray to the Ka'ba."

The group of five gathered close together, and his friend Ahmed said in English, "Anything, brother Ibrahim. We are so bonded right now, bro. We have made it! Speak your heart, brother."

The men all smiled and welcomed him to speak.

"I don't even remember exactly how long it's been since we've known each other," he began. "But I feel something special in my heart, and I've even begun feeling more comfortable with my beard."

"It is not bad for an American infidel," Ahmed said, and the friends all laughed.

More tears began to flow from Cardinal's eyes, only now out of shame and not happiness. "Brothers, I am not who I say I am."

The smiles of his friends were suddenly replaced with looks of concern.

"My real name is John, John Cardinal...." he continued. "I'm not a college student, never was.... I'm not quite sure how to say this, but... I'm actually a CIA agent, assigned to monitor you all.... I am sorry to have deceived you, my brothers, but now... now I have seen the light...."

But his friends were no longer listening to him. They were all too preoccupied staring at something in the sky.

Some of the other Muslims near the Ka'ba were looking up and pointing at the sky as well.

There was something falling down toward them. Something heading straight for the Ka'ba.

Some in the crowd screamed that it was an angel, and others cried that it was a devil, but Agent Cardinal recognized it to be a man.

When the parachute finally opened, Agent Cardinal was able to make out his face. It was none other than the leader of ISIS himself, Abu Bakr al-Baghdadi, and his body was strapped with explosives.

He landed right on top of the Ka'ba.

The German Muslims went from a sense of bewilderment over Agent Cardinal's confession to one of righteous rage at the man who dared to tred upon the holiest of holy.

Agent Cardinal eyed his friends apprehensively. Whether they would harm him or not, he did not know, but it was obvious to all who were present that Bakr was there to cause harm.

He watched the leader of ISIS parade around on top of the Ka'ba, threatening those below with TNT and C-4. It reminded Cardinal of a scene from one of his favorite films, *The Dark Knight*, where the Joker visits the other crime lords.

"No, I am not an angel," Bakr said in Arabic to the crowd, "but I *am* from Allah!"

Shocked out of their silence, the crowd surrounding the

Ka'ba began booing at him. They called him everything from heretic to fat ass, but he shook his finger 'no' and then signaled for them to be silent.

They only yelled louder until Bakr began fingering the cord attached to his vest of explosives.

"I'll pull it!" he screamed. "I'll pull it if you don't show your Caliph the proper respect!"

Muslims from all over the world submitted to his demand. Some fell silent out of fear, and others out of religious duty to protect the Ka'ba.

Bakr smiled. He always did enjoy being in the spotlight. One of his favorite things to do was leading the prayers at the mosque in Raqqa, his capital city, but there was something about an angry mob that made him feel most alive.

Before he became the leader of ISIS, Bakr had been a soccer star in the making. He had a corner shot that was blessed by Allah himself, and field awareness he'd inherited from the great Mesopotamian warriors. He never got along with his teammates, but it didn't matter because of what he could do on the field.

A soccer career could have led Bakr to a life of peace, travel, and joy for himself and others, but alas his game was far from perfect. His lack of speed and his weakness on defense ultimately kept him from competing in Europe. Depressed and disheartened, he found solace in Islamic Studies at Baghdad University, a college known for its mathematics program and extracurricular activities involving the stoning of raped women and homosexuals.

He fit in well there, much more so than he ever did with his soccer teams. As it turned out, he was far better at memorizing passages from the Quran and the Hadith than the strategies of goalkeepers.

After a few years at ISBU, he was a top student writing his thesis on what would eventually become the underlying ideology of ISIS. He no longer missed playing soccer and firmly believed that, like most things in the modern world, it was corrupted and controlled by the Americans and the Jews.

All was corrupted.

The only way to cleanse the world for Bakr was to bring about the apocalypse. Through his studies, he determined that the only way to usher in Judgment Day was for a new Caliph to claim territory under True Islam, thus ending this age of Jahiliyyah—the time of ignorance.

Bakr claimed this truth within himself. He was the man to rule the Caliphate, believing that Allah himself had bestowed these revelations upon him. The members of ISIS believed he held the divine right of Caliph, but the Muslims by the Ka'ba saw only a man driven by hubris and hatred.

"My fellow brothers of Islam!" Bakr cried, addressing the crowd with arms raised high. "I know you have been lost in these times of Jahiliyyah, but, my brothers, you now have a new Caliph, one who claims this Ka'ba in the name of Allah. It is time to begin our worldwide Jihad, spilling the blood of this godless world in sacrifice to Allah. Bow to me, for I am your Caliph! Follow me into most glorious Jihad! Allah Hu Akbar!"

The crowd began to boo at Bakr once again.

In response, he simply laughed and said, "You are all heretics, blinded by liberal Islam. You do not even recognize your true Caliph, and for this you shall perish!"

A collective gasp arose from the crowd as he pressed a button on his vest, but there was no great explosion.

Seeing no visible effect, the crowd only laughed and jeered at the buffoon.

"*You* are the heretic!" a man from Iran screamed in Farsi.

Many of the assembled Muslims yelled in agreement, but the leader of ISIS stood proud, smiling triumphantly, just like he used to do after a successful penalty kick.

The jeering crowd grew louder and angrier. Many of the Muslim men teased the ISIS leader, but Agent Cardinal was not among them. He could tell by the terrorist's confident poise that he had something sinister up his sleeve. Something bad. Agent Cardinal had read Bakr's entire file, recalling the bit about how he liked to play soccer with the heads of wanton women, homosexuals, and liberal Muslims.

This man was truly ruthless in every definition of the word.

"Brothers, we must go," Cardinal said to his friends. "We have to go now! This man is about to unleash something terrible; we must leave this place at once! *He* is the real terrorist, not you my brothers."

They all remained silent, skeptical of his intentions.

"I am sorry, my brothers," he continued. "I hope and I pray, Inshallah, that one day you will forgive me. But for right now, you must follow me if you want to live!"

The men just shook their heads in disgust.

"Follow you where?" Ahmed asked. "To Guantanamo Bay? Your fear in the face of this madness shows that you were never a true Muslim to begin with. You do not have real faith, which comes as no surprise, as no scumbag American CIA *liar* could ever hope to see the real truth. A *true* Muslim would feel the protection of Allah when standing before the great Ka'ba."

"I *do* have faith," Agent Cardinal protested, "but if we don't leave now…."

The ground beneath them began to rumble. Whatever Bakr had planned for them, it was about to happen, and even Allah would not be able to stop it.

"RUNNNN!!!" Cardinal screamed, turning to do just that.

Only someone grabbed his shoulder before he could get away.

"No," Ahmed said, his voice now rumbling with the ground they stood upon. "Whatever is going to happen, we experience it as *brothers*. As Muslims, as brothers in faith. If you are a true Muslim, stay with us and trust Allah to let us live or take us all to paradise!"

The others nodded solemnly in agreement.

Cardinal stopped and thought about the loved ones he still had back home. His twin brother who worked for the President, the family he hoped to one day start, and even the luxurious

American way of life he still missed every now and then. He honestly wasn't sure if he was ready to die just yet.

But if he had to go today, he wanted to go as Ibrahim, not as John Cardinal.

"Okay," he said, "whatever happens, I will be with my brothers. With my fellow Muslims! Live or die, we are all in Allah's hands now. Inshallah."

The group shared a somber look and embraced. Forming a circle, they stuck their heads close together and said as one, "Inshallah."

They stayed huddled together like that for some time, and Cardinal had even begun to feel the love and forgiveness of Ibrahim's true friends and brothers, but that blissful moment of spiritual unity was unfortunately cut short.

Every Muslim in the area screamed in terror at what emerged from the sand all around them.

"SHARKS!!!"
"SIMK ALQARSH!!!
"ASMAK ALQURSH!!!"
"REQUIN!!!"
In every human tongue represented by the Ka'ba that day,

their adversary was named.

Only these weren't normal sharks, bound by nature or their need for water. These were cybernetic sharks that swam in sand with human-like faces.

Agent Cardinal remembered looking into the X-Files on Singularity terrorism. He remembered one file in particular that had been so ridiculous it stayed with him, some garbage about how terrorists were trying to migrate consciousness into mechanical devices intertwined with their bodies, or even better yet, the bodies of more powerful animals, for the purpose of carrying out the largest must brutal terrorist attack the world had ever seen.

It sounded so ridiculous that the agents had even made it into a running joke around the office. However, when Cardinal caught sight of all the shark fins cutting through the sand, he knew that there was nothing more to laugh about.

Singularity terrorism was real, and these sharks were the proof.

Moving with incredible speed, they dipped down and leapt up from the sand, swimming more like dolphins than sharks. Each time they emerged, they revealed the azure-blue ISIS symbols adorning their metal-plated bodies. These were not merely etched or tattooed upon them. Rather, they were a physical manifestation of their terrorist consciousness, glowing with faint, pulsing light.

But the absolute worst was their faces.

Row upon row of long, razor-sharp teeth protruded from their grotesque, humanoid heads. Agent Cardinal recognized a few of those faces as belonging to top-level members of ISIS.

"ISIS Sharks of Singularity!" he cried out in horror.

"Yes, they are!" Bakr proclaimed, still standing atop the Ka'ba. "Allah Hu Akbar! Feast upon the infidels!"

"ALLAH HU AKBAR," the sharks all droned as one, their booming mechanical voice a weapon in itself.

For technically being Muslim sharks, they certainly had very little love for their Muslim brethren, and those who took to their knees in prayer were the first to be devoured.

The ISIS Sharks of Singularity harbored an insatiable hunger for human flesh, but they'd been programmed to eat only non-ISIS members. Circling the crowd of Muslims gathered around the Ka'ba, they were not just eating for sustenance, but also for sport.

The leader of ISIS looked on as innocent Muslims were brutally slaughtered by creatures far worse than any drone. He smiled, clapped, and cried out at the top of his lungs, "YES!!! Jihad on them, my brothers!"

Bakr looked down at Agent Cardinal and his friends. "Allah has seen fit to join his greatest natural creatures with his greatest spiritual warriors. My men get something even *better* than a holy death; they get eternal life as Allah's own killing machines right here on Earth! Allah Hu Akbar!"

Agent Cardinal glanced back at the sharks, who were rapidly thinning the herd. Leaping from sand hole to sand hole, they ruthlessly decapitated those they saw as infidels, just as they had in human life.

As the sharks squeezed the crowd ever tighter, it became increasingly clear that there was nowhere left to run. These were the last moments of his and his friends' lives.

"Brothers," Cardinal said, "I am ready to die a true Muslim. I am ready to die with the only true friends I have ever had."

Ahmed nodded and the others agreed. As the sharks bore down upon them, the men joined hands and said their final prayers.

With his last thoughts, Ibrahim said to Allah, I go to you with clean heart and mind. I go knowing that this was not your doing, Oh Lord. No, this was the act of a truly evil being....

Chapter 3

Trump Island: Undisclosed Location

Slowly descending from the sky, three bulletproof choppers touched down upon a giant helipad that read: YOU'RE FIRED. Each of them had a different nation's flag mounted on their respective tail wings, proudly waving in the balmy breeze.

Donald Trump walked out from the beachside bungalow where he had his daily brunch.

"They are here," he said, addressing his servants. "Get us some mimosas with sake, vodka, and some 'jungle joo joo', or baby blood, whatever the hell it is those Africans drink over there. This is big stuff, guys. Big stuff, not just boardroom, but global. Major deals. Major players."

As he said this, Presidents Xi Jinping of China, Vladimir

Putin of Russia, and Yoweri Museveni of Uganda each exited their respective helicopters.

Trump was very pleased to see them but kept himself from smiling. Negotiations hadn't even started yet, and a welcoming smile was the surest way of showing weakness. With his usual squinty-eyed scowl, he went forth to greet his guests, giving them each a brisk nod as he approached.

The helicopter blades hadn't stopped spinning yet, but Trump's trademark hair stayed perfectly in place. Often before crucial deals and big meetings with the big dogs, his stylists would apply a little extra mouse, and today was going to be the biggest deal of Trump's life.

Turning his steely gaze away from the world leaders, he glanced out at the shore. The words "Trump Island" had been written in the colors of the Tibetan flag across the beach with sacred sand. The sight of it upset Trump because it hadn't been done by real Tibetan monks.

Trump didn't care for their politics or their notions of peace, nor did he desire state autonomy for the long-oppressed Tibetans. He wanted the best sand designs money could buy, and he always enjoyed pissing off China.

The first time the real Tibetan monks had completed their sand mural, Trump was pleased. It was gorgeous and worth every penny he'd paid for it. He clapped and congratulated them. The Tibetans smiled, bowed, and then proceeded to kick their creation to the winds, destroying all the work they had just done.

Trump was livid and couldn't believe what he saw. He didn't understand it, nor did he care that it was intended as a Tibetan celebration of impermanence. He had human-trafficked these monks all the way from Asia, and he expected them to do their god damn job.

He demanded that they begin from scratch right then and there. The monks politely declined.

"No!" Trump shouted, his face turning bright red. "You fix that fucking sand or I'll make you pay in ways that will make you forget everything you've ever learned from your precious Buddha."

The Buddhists remained silent and still.

"If you won't do your job, I won't just fire you," the billionaire told the monks, "I'll get China to turn all of Tibet into one big Apple sweatshop! Jesus, you people are dumber than Mexicans. You *are* going to do this job over, understood?"

Trump called his security guards and Omarosa, his protégé and personal assistant from *The Apprentice*, over to assist him.

"Detain these losers," he instructed, "and bring them down to Kurzweil in the aquarium lab. Monks... yeah, right. More like panhandle artists putting diapers on piss clams. Losers."

"You heard the man," Omarosa barked. "Move!"

Trump believed that everyone had a price. He felt that in his core. It was a principle he'd internalized since he was a young boy, and one he would later build his future success upon.

The guards took the passive monks in hand, taking them to a lab America never would have allowed to exist.

Trump followed them there, smiling smugly as he watched the expression on the monks' faces go from stoicism to sheer horror.

They'd never felt fear like this before, even while being

tortured by the Chinese, but what they witnessed in the lab was far worse than any torture they could imagine. These were abominations so unreal, so unnatural, they perverted the very laws of Dharma, science, and life itself.

The creatures in the tanks before them had undergone procedures so twisted as to turn them into hulking beasts. Part man, part shark, part robot, and all killing machine. Their red, rage-filled eyes said it all.

They wanted to eat, or they wanted die.

Trump loved the sight of the creatures he'd created, but he loved seeing the horrified Buddhists even more.

"Okay fellas," he said, "now, you are either going to do another one of your pretty sand design things, or you are going to be my next specimens to go in the tank."

Several of the monks had begun to cry, holding each other close in their saffron robes.

"Those things you seen in there?" Trump said, pointing to the nearest tank. "They were once top porn stars; they had heavy appetites for flesh as humans, even worse now as sharks...."

The monks all trembled with fear, imagining the horrors of sharing a tank with such obscene monstrosities.

"Come to think of it," Trump continued, "it would be interesting to see how *you* guys would work as Singularity sharks.... I know you losers don't believe in a self or whatever, but rest assured, you will have a whole new concept of that after you enter these tanks."

The sobbing monks looked at Trump with pleading eyes, shaking their heads 'no'.

Trump threw his hands up in frustration.

"Fine," he said. "Buncha mute jerks. You think you're *sooo* good, you don't even have to talk, thinking you'll be rewarded with dumplings and dogs to eat when you're reincarnated, but I'll be saving you the trip. You'll be trapped in *this* life forever.... Kurzweil, get over here!"

Emerging from the shadows of the dark aquarium, Ray Kurzweil, renowned scientist of Singularity theory, appeared beside him. He wore a white lab coat and a special tracking bracelet Trump had forced upon him following his capture.

"Yes, Mr. Trump?" he asked.

"More specimens here, for your shark-man-Singularity project. Get on it."

"Very well, sir. They will be fun to test on."

"Just do you job. Save your fun for the video games."

Trump just shook his head, annoyed before he'd even had his daily brunch. His phone began to buzz in his front pants pocket.

Taking it out, he saw a text from his agent. He read that he wouldn't be allowed on *Shark Tank*, because his rival Mark Cuban refused to let him come on the show.

Enraged by the news, Trump threw his phone on the floor. "That loser," he said. "He thinks he's Mr. Big Shot just because he can keep me off his stupid TV show? Pathetic. Wait until he gets a load of what's in *my* shark tank...."

Presidents Putin, Museveni, and Jinping followed Trump into his beachside bungalow. They all sat down together at the table on the veranda, ready to discuss business over brunch. The security guards left them alone but Omarosa remained by her master's side.

Before they could begin their meeting, Trump noticed the men ogling his Nukes of Singularity, arranged in neat stacks beside him. Each of the living atomic missiles had been infused with human consciousness, bearded human faces adorning their warhead tips.

"Yes, they are a thing of beauty, aren't they?" Trump said. "Like anyone worthwhile, they only speak when spoken to, but please, gentlemen, let us first enjoy this is five-star brunch to celebrate your arrival."

Trump lifted his mimosa, toasted his guests, and took a sip.

President Jinping took a sip as well, but promptly spat it out. "Is that sake in here? I don't drink that Japanese piss!"

"My mistake, President Jinping," Trump said. He was pleased by his display of dominance, successfully rattling Jinping's temperament. "Omarosa, please bring the Chinese President a champagne mimosa, like mine."

President Jinping wiped his mouth and looked out at the beach. "Ah, I see you use Tibetans to make pretty sand words," he said. "They do same for me, but then they blow all beauty away! It make me so sad, I make them blow me, then I blow up their temple, hahahahaha!"

"We had twelve Buddhists in Uganda," President Museveni said. "No good. We cook them in stew along with homosexuals. Fire kills AIDS in blood, you see. Very delicious."

"Personally, Museveni," Trump said with authority, "I like the gays. They have money like the Jews, but unlike the Jews they actually spend it on things. Good for the economy. Why, a homosexual even designed my trademark hair…."

Truthfully, Trump thought the gays were about as useful to America as Muslims and Mexicans, but he usually liked to follow rule #7 of his bestselling book, *The Art of Deal* – Always take the opposite position of those you are negotiating with.

"I've killed more faggots and Jews than the Inquisition," boasted Putin, downing his entire vodka mimosa. "I don't have time for nonsense talk. Put on TV and let us see how well my ISIS sharks have done, for the Phase 2 of our plan. Trump, have your slave put on the Fox News. I like the O'Reilly…."

Trump saw that Putin was and would always be his main competition, but he remained calm and said, "Put on the TV, Omarosa."

"Hey, Russian prince," Museveni said to Putin. "You no talk to beautiful African princess that way." He grinned widely as he turned to her. "You *much* more beautiful in person than on television. Uganda *loves* you."

Omarosa answered him with a coquettish smile. She may have found Putin slightly off-putting, but the Ugandan President was surprisingly charming. She turned on the TV as ordered and then excused herself into the bungalow.

Putin dug into his omelet with relish while he watched the TV screen. He smiled as he chewed his food, witnessing all the carnage stacked up around the Ka'ba.

"The ISIS sand sharks are following plan very well," he said. "That is thing with terrorists, gentleman. They not so bad once you point them in right direction. All of them very much have same brain like monkey or dog; just train, and then unleash. After these shark-monkeys dominate Middle East and take down Israel, Russia shall rule Middle East and Europe as well. These sharks are best ones I make with Trump. Hey, Jinping," he continued, "you don't even have sharks anymore. American scientists kill them all!"

"Not true, Ruski man," President Jinping retorted, "My Chinese megalodon is Godzilla of sea; my sharks already destroy White House and Obama, too. They even ate up NSA. I did my part, now it Trump's job to conquer rest of world. Hey, Museveni," he continued, "why Uganda no fund special sharks? Because Africa so poor? Hahahahaha! Africans *sooo* stupid...."

"I wish to *buy* special sharks, Chinaman," President Museveni protested, "but cannot afford yet. Give me credit and give me sharks!"

"You want sharks now?" Jinping shot back. "You *pay* now! You pay *now*, Museveni! No credit; I no trust Africans with credit! So you pay now and in *money*, not zebra skins...."

"I already tell you, I don't have money yet," Museveni

responded. He looked over at Putin and continued, "I want *Italy*, President Putin. Russia and China acting like British Empire now, same as before. No fair to Africa!"

"Go cry about it to your witchdoctor," Putin said, still watching the TV. "You get nothing. We give you *Africa*. Be happy you are not slave to sharks."

"NO!!!" boomed Museveni, slamming his fist on the table. "This is racism! I want *more*. I am world leader, too!"

The Ugandan President ceased his tirade when Bill O'Reilly appeared onscreen.

"And as if this day couldn't get even *more* tragic," O'Reilly said, "we have now confirmed that nearly twenty American celebrities have gone missing. We have no idea if this is related to the ISIS sharks or not, but...."

President Putin rolled his eyes and said, "Garbage. U.S. care more about side-boob celebrities than things that matter, like sharks. That is why they will fall, and hard. The truth we all know is I am best man here, so I should be new leader."

"I no care about celebrities," President Museveni protested, "I only want more power. I want to be leader, Trump. Please, you must handle this."

"Wait, *I* should be leader..." Jinping said. "Oooh, wait! One of celebrities missing is J-Law!" He could barely contain his excitement. "I must tell you, I not do *one* act of governance on day of glorious Fappening!" He then proceeded to mime vigorous masturbation and ejaculating everywhere.

Everyone at the table appeared discontent with the exception of Trump, who wore a wry smile on his face. He was thinking of rule 17 in his book – The best man for the job should always get it.

"Gentleman," he began, "now that we've put some excellent food in our stomachs and we've toasted to our plan, I want you all to follow me outside. I've arranged a challenge for us that will settle our disagreements in a productive and enjoyable manner."

The world leaders followed Trump down the sandy beach and into the palm trees, marveling at the waterfalls and exotic birds all around. None of them had ever seen such natural beauty in their own homelands.

They were also quite impressed by all the missile silos tastefully dotting the landscape. Trump was proud of the Feng Shui he'd put into the design. Even President Jinping was pleased by this use of the ancient Chinese art.

It was indeed an impressive island on its surface, but not half as impressive as the secrets held within.

Only Trump, Jeffrey Epstein, select world leaders, and the top 1% of the 1% richest billionaires even knew of the island's existence. This small handful of men and women would often use the secret territory as a vacation spot, holding underage sex parties there, making highly illegal business deals, and last but not least, hunting human beings.

The hunting on Trump Island became such a popular staple that when a deal couldn't be reached in the boardroom, it would usually be settled in the jungle. The winner of each hunt won the right to make decisions for the New World Order for that quarter.

These secret meetings were held four times each year, and guests were only allowed to bring their most useless of servants.

Whenever the business leaders disagreed, Trump would say, "On Trump Island, the greatest hunters are those who lead the world. Here, we make the *ultimate* deal. We follow natural law on this island, as we should and always have, capisce? Gather your servants, and whoever bags the most gets the deal."

Not surprisingly, Trump Island became the most sought-after destination of the ruling class from business moguls to top politicians. The Koch brothers and Chancellor Merkel came one time to hold EU trade discussions, killing all of Merkel's assistants in the process.

The Koch brothers won, like usual.

Today, however, Trump had planned a special game for his guests, because the stakes were so high.

Leading their way through the jungle, he took the Presidents past the koi pond where the Koch brothers had raped and dismembered the FIFA director's laziest ball boys. Trump didn't much care for witnessing these wicked acts, but on Trump Island there was no morality observed, only the laws of nature.

"It so *hot* out here..." whined Jinping. "Why we not stay in shade of bungalow, drinking piña coladas instead?"

"We no celebrate," Museveni retorted. "I no have Italy or

Spain. And don't give me Greece. Even Africa feels bad for that country."

Putin shook his head and said, "I deserve all. Russia has most successful sharks. Russia best, always."

"Gentleman, please stop for a second," Trump said. "Let's lay it all on the table. None of us want to be in second place. We all see ourselves as winners. Well, except for Uganda, but that's just nature. There've been studies."

"Hey, that was imperialism," Museveni shot back. "It is—"

"Let me finish," Trump cut him off. "We need a fair way to decide who is in charge of our little group, and also your sharks are not the best, President Putin. *Mine* are. The truth is that it doesn't matter what we think, it matters what we *do*. We all believe we are the best and I know I am, but I am also a fair man, gentlemen, and when my father lent me money I failed *four* times before I succeeded–because greatness never quits."

"What is the point of this foolish speech, Trump?" Putin asked.

"The point is that we need to decide who is in charge, who will be the leader of our alliance. And we will decide the same way we've always decided on Trump Island."

"Can it be movie trivia?" Jinping asked.

"No," Trump said with a smile. "Let's just say that it will involve a test of strength, but not just the physical variety. Right this way, gentlemen...."

The four men of power trudged through the jungle until they reached a golden placard, sunk into the trunk of a towering palm. HUNTING GROUNDS, it read.

Past the sign was an array of tropical foliage that had been landscaped to form an elaborate hedge maze to inspire psychological terror.

Before the entrance to the hunting grounds stood a large, metal containment unit. There were no openings in this structure save for the thinnest of ventilation slits, to keep its captives from suffocating. Muffled pleas for mercy could be heard echoing from within.

Several of Trump's servants stood nearby, each of them carting wheelbarrows loaded with weapons. The Presidents all smiled at the selection placed before them.

"Alright, men," Trump began. "First, some rules."

"I like rules," Putin interjected. "Rules are the foundation of a strong society. Go on, Trump."

"These gifts I give to you, you will hunt," Trump said, "and he who scores the most kills becomes leader of our alliance. We only hunt our prey, not each other. There are video cameras set up all throughout this jungle, so please rest assured that you will be executed on the spot if such an act is even attempted."

The President of Uganda raised his hand and Trump rolled his eyes. "Speak," he said.

"Mr. Trump," Museveni began, "for alliance, we still have no name. We must have strong name, for our alliance."

"Our name should be, This is Stupid Fucking Question," Putin said. "Whatever we hunt today, I will kill easily."

"I like the attitude, Putin," said Trump. "So, let's get to it. Winner runs the show here and assumes control over the world territories of their choosing. That is how all business deals are decided on Trump Island. Now, let us see your presents, shall we? Open the gates!"

"I hope it is goats," Museveni said.

"Even better," Trump replied with a smile.

All at once, the shocked Presidents recalled the news regarding those missing celebrities.

Trump had taken them.

As it turned out, all nineteen individual cells contained prisoners so famous that even these men of power felt star-struck in their presence. Half naked and starved, these were the only people on Earth whose fame and financial earnings came even close to approaching their own.

The roster of prisoners included:

1)   Robert Griffin III (or RG3 for short), Ex-QB for the Washington Redskins

2)   Larry David, creator of TV's *Seinfeld*

3)   Jennifer Lawrence, star of the *Hunger Games* series and the Fappening

4)   Adrian Brody, Academy Award-winning actor

5)   Arnold Schwarzenegger, former Mr. Universe and Governater

6)   Aaron Rodgers, quarterback for the Green Bay Packers

7)   Katy Perry, pop singer and one of Forbes' Top-Earning Women in Music

8)   Kobe Bryant, shooting guard for the Los Angeles Lakers and alleged rapist

9)   Kevin Hart, short black comedian

10) Stephen Hawking, acclaimed astrophysicist

11) Jesse Ventura, former pro wrester, Governor of Minnesota, and conspiracy theorist

12) Danny Glover, venerable actor, director, and political activist

13) Carl Weathers, from *Rocky*, *Rocky II*, and the *Predator* films

14-19) The entire cast of TV's *Shark Tank* (Kevin O'Leary, Barbara Corcoran, Daymond John, Robert Herjavec, Lori Greiner, and Mark Cuban)

Trump raised his arms up in victory. "These are your primary targets, gentlemen," he proudly proclaimed. "Athletes, singers, annoying comedians, actresses, geniuses, the stars from the *Predator* films, and everyone on *Shark Tank*. I'll admit, that last one is personal, but they should still be fun for us all to kill. This shall be the most glorious Trump Island hunt yet, a contest to prove which one of us shall lead the world after the great Sharkpocaylpse!"

"God... America..." Schwarzenegger grunted. "Someone, please, help us!"

"Ha!" Jinping sneered. "America too busy being eaten by megalodon sharks. They can no help you now, hahaha! My megalodons eat all Americans, just like you eat hamburgers and your hot dogs. This so fun, I can't wait to kill J-Law...."

Jennifer Lawrence was full of rage, almost like she was acting in one of her films. "Fuck you, you loser Leslie Chow-sounding asshole!" she spat. "I survived the *Hunger Games* and the Fappening. America will save us and stop your stupid-ass sharks!"

"This is all about me not letting you on *Shark Tank*, isn't it?!" Mark Cuban yelled at Trump. "Well, I've got news for you, jerk. America will survive your sharks and lay the heavy hand of justice as well as the long dick of the law on all you crazy butt-fuckers!"

"*Shark Tank* was a show with nothing but losers," Trump replied, scowling. "And America won't be saving anyone after they see what's in *my* shark tank!"

ACT 2

Chapter 4

Open Water: Washington, D.C.

Admiral Rodgers watched in horror as the mother megalodon devoured Gaddafi's girls whole, leaving him and the others defenseless on deck. He had been on under-attack ships before, and he knew that there were really only two rules in this situation— find a weapon, and save a few breaths to pray to your maker.

Gaddafi ran up to him, Hillary, and Tea Time. There were thick tears of anger running down the deep creases of his face.

"That bitch ate my guards!" he howled in anguish. "What will we do now?"

They were joined by Condoleezza, Bill, and Epstein, but the playboy pedophile had nothing but a lousy martini in hand.

"Where are your weapons?" the Admiral demanded to know.

"Ummm, felons aren't allowed to have them," Epstein replied. "Not legally, anyway...."

Gaddafi took Condoleezza's hand. "I am afraid to die," he admitted to her. "Like, for real this time. My girls may be gone, but with you, my African princess, at least I can die feeling like a true African king."

Bill Clinton caught this and placed his hand on his wife's shoulder. "Baby, you have been a good wife," he said, "putting up with all my shenanigans. If you wanna reenact that scene from *Titanic* before we die, I would do it just for you."

"What?!" Hillary snapped back, slapping his hand away. "I don't want a romantic dying moment; I want to live and stop these terrorist sharks!"

"We must live, Madam President," the Admiral said. "Because it's not just ISIS sharks we need to worry about, but also Donald Trump! He's planning—"

"Trump?" Epstein cut him off. "That's my man! What's he up to? We should definitely head over to Trump Island for whatever he has in mi—"

Losing his cool, Roberts punched him in the face. "Not only has that island been experimenting with ISIS sharks and hosting sex rings for billionaires," he said, looking to Hillary, "but we have intel that they now have nuclear missiles with sentient, cybernetic properties. Little here uncovered the whole plot! It's all connected."

Tea Time nodded his head with confidence, but in truth he was pissing his pants at the prospect of the next shark attack.

"I didn't know what he was doing out there!" Epstein protested, rubbing his sore jaw. "Geez, he just gave me a place to party! Bill, you probably wouldn't like the hunting out there, but the *girls*, oh man...."

Cocking back her fist, Hillary punched Epstein in the face. "Shut up and do as I say," she said to the group. "We need to do two things within the next two minutes. First, we must stop that big-ass shark, and second," she continued, looking at Epstein, "you little twerp pedo twat-sniffer, *you* are going to lead us to Trump Island so we can put an end to whatever that shitty-haired son of a cunt has in mind."

"Fine," Tea Time said, "but what about this fucking shark? And how the fuck are we supposed to stop it?"

Everyone fell silent then, which in D.C. translates to, "I don't know."

The mother megalodon had been sated for the moment, but she was still feeling far from satisfied. Burping up the occasional bikini or assault rifle now and then, she swam in nervous circles deep beneath the hull of the *Jailbaiter*.

Her hunger wasn't just about food, but vengeance for all her dead babies. And as if their spilled blood wasn't enough to send her into primal rage, she was now picking up the pheromones of another female shark in the area.

The Chinese scientists had given her heightened senses and awareness, modeling their approach after the film *Deep Blue Sea*, but their methods had been far from perfect. The megalodon understood the connection between the yacht and the slaughter of her children, but these pheromones were coming from somewhere else.

Megalodon sharks weren't exactly known for getting nervous.

Instinctually she could tell that the other shark wasn't any bigger than her, but there was something different about its hormonal structure that made it especially dangerous.

As more and more of her dead babies sunk down to her, the mother megalodon's fear was eclipsed by a resurgence of anger. Her stomach felt a bit upset by all those bikinis and breast implants she'd swallowed, but there was still enough room for the rest of the humans on that ship.

Shooting back up to the surface, she was tempted to ram the *Jailbaiter* from underneath. Instead, she whipped around and launched herself over its side.

"OH SHIT!!!" screamed Tea Time, watching the giant shark sail toward him with its jaws open wide. "FUUUUCK, we're all gonna—"

CHOMP!!!

Tea Time was bit in two before he could even finish his sentence, his upper half joining Gaddafi's guards in the giant shark's stomach.

"LITTLE!!!" Rodgers cried in anguish.

Landing on deck with a tremendous crash, the mother megalodon nearly sank them right then and there. Hilary and the Admiral were knocked down by the impact, while the others onboard scattered to the stern of the ship.

The Admiral didn't fear death, but he certainly feared those nukes on Trump Island. His own death was nothing, but the death of the world was something he could not accept.

Watching as the shark's teeth came gashing toward them, Hillary *did* fear her own death, but what she feared even more was failing at her turn as President. She wanted to be revered by the history books for averting the Sharkpocalypse, not for being killed on her first day of duty.

Hillary and the Admiral closed their eyes and held each other tight, awaiting their imminent ends.

"Duck motherfuckers!" someone yelled from out on the water. "I'm makin' shark fin soup, my nigga!"

Before the mother megalodon could close its jaws around them, a bazooka blast hit her right in the side of the head. Large chunks of megalodon meat rained down upon the deck, showering all onboard with gobs of blood and brain matter.

"HELP!!!" Hillary screamed to whoever it was who'd saved them. "Help us, we're sinking!"

"That's two miracles in one day," the Admiral muttered. "Maybe there really is a God after all…."

Only it wasn't God at all, but a man in a dingy with a bazooka.

Looking overboard, they saw that he was tall, bald, and

African-American. He held a missile launcher slung over his shoulder in one hand, puffing on a cigarette with the other. Both Hillary and the Admiral found him to be vaguely familiar. They had seen his face before, but they couldn't place exactly where.

As the dingy pulled up alongside the rapidly foundering *Jailbaiter*, its crew finally noticed the cruise ship in the distance.

"Who are you?" Gaddafi yelled overboard. "Who is it that's saved us?"

"Yo ass been saved by DMX," replied the once-famous rapper. "Where my dogs at? Hurry, hop on my ride, before that shit sinks." As he spoke, it almost sounded like he was rapping at them.

Bill Clinton recognized his voice instantly, giving him a thumbs up over the side of the yacht. "DMX, what up son?" he drawled in his soft, gravelly voice. "Harlem love, brother."

"Oh shit, Bill Clinton!" DMX replied, just as surprised as everyone else. "What's good, my nigga? Shit, I just saved the motherfucking forty-second President of the United States!"

"And the forty-fifth..." Hilary mumbled under her breath.

"And these niggas be talkin' shit that DMX is washed up," the rapper continued, "that I'm a crackhead n' shit. What y'all really want! A hero, that's what you niggas want, and I just saved the president."

"I love your songs about dogs, son," Bill said with a smile, "and that's *two* presidents you just saved, my wife and myself."

"I don't back down from sharks," DMX replied. "If LL Cool J could kill a shark with a little ol' cross like in that movie, I could kill that *big* motherfucker with this here bazooka. Y'all lucky I was in the neighborhood!"

"Mr. X, you have our undying gratitude" Hillary said as she looked the rapper over. "I will see that you are awarded the Congressional Medal of Honor. But can I ask what you're doing out here, and where you got that bazooka?"

"I'm workin' security these days," he replied, looking somewhat ashamed. "Shit's whack, son. Back when your husband was runnin' shit, my pockets were as fat as the asses in all my videos. Now, the Industry got no love for DMX no more, and I still got priors! So, these new-school, cheesy-ass Miami niggas T-Pain, Flo Rida, and Pitbull hired me to do security for their cruise tour; we was hittin' up the Potomac when this storm and shark shit happened. Ain't so bad, though; they got some bitches onboard whose moms were down with my shit back in tha day, and I been killing *a lot* of motherfuckin' sharks for they asses. Keeps a nigga outta trouble, so I don't mind."

"You're an American hero, Mr. X," Hillary said.

DMX looked contemplative and asked, "Does this mean y'all can take care of my priors?"

"You get us off this yacht and onto that cruise ship," she replied, "and I'll give you full immunity!"

The survivors of the sunken *Jailbaiter* boarded the rappers' cruise ship. Flo Rida's "Going Down For Real" was bumping on the sound system as they walked up the gangplank.

The boat was small as far as cruise ships went, but just as extravagant as any Royal Caribbean line. It even boasted a retractable roof, to keep to party going even during hurricanes.

Hillary and her crew followed DMX to the upper deck of the ship. It had an Olympic-sized pool full of girls who didn't even seem to notice there'd been a massive storm and shark epidemic. Many of these attractive young women of various nationalities had what appeared to be cocaine dusting their nostrils.

Bill gave a thumbs up to all the girls and Hillary just shook her head, annoyed that even in the midst of this crisis, her husband remained focused on pussy.

Bill took his eyes off the pool girls for a moment and noticed that there were a bunch of white, twenty- to thirty-something hipsters dancing badly nearby. He had a certain fondness for the hot hipster girls, but the bearded men with non-prescription glasses and PBR tallboys unfortunately outnumbered them.

"Yo, X," Bill said to the rapper. "Hey bruh, what's with all these squares on the ship? I thought this was supposed to be some dope hip hop cruise."

"Shit man, the recording industry is dead, B. Besides gettin' cash for commercials, ain't no money in music anymore. These Miami herb niggas bought a party cruise from Miami to D.C. They be dancing like some retarded-ass zombies n' shit, all up on some blog shit called Buzzfeed. Can't stand these nerdy herb-ass niggas. They always be makin' lists, yo. Sayin' snide-ass shit about me behind my back. They lucky I'm on parole. You know what I'm sayin', B?"

"Can't the stand the media, bruh," Bill Clinton agreed, emphasizing his Harlem inflection. "I like these young girls with the asymmetrical hair cuts, though. They got any vegan quesadillas on this ship?"

"Eh, still too old for me," Epstein chimed in.

"That motherfucker ain't right," DMX said and shook his head.

"Where is Mr. Rida, Pain, and Bull? Hillary asked. "We require passage to a secret island, STAT. It is a matter of national security."

"T-Pain right here motherfucker," T-Pain said as he approached, sipping on some cough syrup. "Who you be, you pirate-ass-lookin' bitch?"

"I am the President of the United States," Hillary said.

"*Dayaaamn*," T-Pain said as his eyes went wide, "I *thought* you was some Clinton-lookin' motherfuckers. I be buggin', yo. Sipping too hard on this here syrup, nah mean? I swear the TV be showin' sand sharks n' shit where them Muslims be." He took another sip of his Robitussin. "The news be sayin' them sharks is headin' toward Israel. End Times, y'all. I went to Church, I know that biblical shit...."

The Admiral nodded his head and said, "Our intel has confirmed that Israel is their prime target."

"Mr. Pain," Hillary said, "this a direct order from me, your President. I'm afraid we must commandeer this ship and head straight to Trump Island. There is no time to lose. Epstein, you give him the coordinates."

"I dunno..." T-Pain said, "I swear I saw me some sharks with big ol' titties in the water earlier, but I be buggin'.... We should probably find safety, ya heard me?"

"I heard nothing," Hillary shot back. "You need to hear *me* and understand that we taking over this ship. Admiral, you go man the helm. Epstein, prove that you are not a complete waste of space and give him the coordinates. We need to get to Trump Island and we need to get there now!"

"What about Israel, Madam President?" Condoleezza asked. "They are our greatest ally in the region, and they might need our assistance with those terrorist Singularity sharks heading their way."

Hillary did have much love for Israel and its people, but she was forced to make a tough decision.

"Israel is on its own, Condie," she said. "Hopefully there really is a God, and they really are His chosen people, because they will need divine intervention if they hope to stop the ISIS sharks."

Chapter 5

War Room: Avant, Israel

"I can't get ahold of the Americans," Prime Minister Benjamin Netanyahu told his cabinet officials. "Just like the Saudis, they too have been attacked by these fucking sharks. This is madness! I never thought I'd say this, but even the Saudis are our allies now. We need all the friends we can get! Hell, hopefully even the Iranians can give us a hand with these ISIS sharks."

His Chief of Staff, Gadi Eizenkot, nodded skeptically. "Maybe," he said, "but I still think the Iranians would rather be eaten by sharks before they'd help us. Same with the Saudis. We are alone, Prime Minister, just like we have always been."

"Fuck me... this is a perversion," Netanyahu replied. "Man, shark, Muslim, and machine. Maybe the Christians are right?

Maybe there really is an end of times, and this is it."

The other cabinet members remained silent. They'd been prepared for talks on dirty bombs or even germ warfare, but certainly not ISIS sand sharks. This particular type of crisis was simply not covered in Israel's counter-terrorism protocol.

One of the intelligence workers, Roth Wineberg, looked up from his computer. "We have intel that the sharks are targeting all key cities in the Middle East," he said. "Their final stop is said to be Jerusalem, where they hope to claim the holy city and bring about… and I quote the ISIS chatrooms… a Sharkocaust."

"Great, now we're dealing *Nazi* Muslim sharks," Netanyahu said, shaking his head in disbelief. "Jesus Christ…. We have no allies, no Jesus, no messiah, but we *do* have our Mossad and other defense networks. Israel has the best homeland security in the world, even better than the Americans! With our special forces and our air force combined, we can at least bring the fight to these sharks before they conquer all of Israel. Like anything of this world, they can be killed."

"But, they aren't really of this world, sir," Wineberg said. "We don't even know for a fact that they *can* be killed."

Netanyahu shrugged nihilistically. "Maybe," he said. "I don't know. One thing I do know, our defenses are top notch. They are programmed to adapt to any threat. Even against the ISIS Sharks of Singularity, we'll still have a better chance with our technology than the Arabs and Persians. Those fools may not realize it, but it is only us Jews and the Asians who are capable of handling such advanced technology. But some asshole gave our secrets over to the ISIS. Motherfuckers!"

The Prime Minister slammed his fist on the table to emphasize his point.

"Those imbeciles still think it's 800 AD," he continued. "There's no way they could've figured out how to transform into mechanical man-sharks on their own. No way! We don't have proof yet, but I bet it was the Russians. They hate us almost as much as the gays. I never did trust Putin. He always reminded me of someone who sells life insurance to the elderly...."

It was then that the Prime Minister's secretary entered the room. She looked meekly at him and said, "I know you said that you couldn't be bothered, but it is your wife, sir. She wanted to speak to you before... umm... she says it is urgent and... she just needs to hear your voice."

"Jesus," Netanyahu replied. "This is why a woman can't be Prime Minister! Okay..." he grumbled as he rose from his seat. "I'll be right back. We must keep in mind what matters in life, or we are just like the mongrels outside our borders."

The Prime Minister walked out of the room and got on his private line.

He did not give a shit about his wife and had many mistresses he would call before her, but he knew that "I need to hear your voice" was really code for "there is a traitor in the room."

He picked up the phone and spoke in code, "Hello dear, how are you?" (Who is the traitor?)

"Fine, I'm so-so," (I don't know, but they are a cabinet member,) replied the voice on the other end.

"Do you think vitamins would help?" (Do they have a bomb?)

"No, but I have constipation." (No, but they are seeking to disrupt our security systems.)

"Okay dear, I must go now. Feel better." (I have to go now. What do I do?)

"Just don't stress about it." (You must figure out who it is before it is too late.)

The Prime Minister hung up the phone and sighed. He had absolutely no idea who the traitor could be.

The head of Israeli Communications, Elijah Rothstein, sat waiting for the Prime Minister to return. He was not schizophrenic, but he'd been hearing the voice again.

The voice was not his conscience. It was alien and computerized and forced him to do things he had no desire to do. It dominated him the way he dominated his opponents on the chessboard.

Rothstein was Israel's most famous scientist, chess superstar, and overall Renaissance man. The epitome of good health and how to live a great life. He had been on the cover of Israeli *GQ* three times.

Not one for leisure and boredom, when he hit sixty-five he only semi-retired. Shortly thereafter, he decided to write a book on the life and work of Ray Kurzweil, a prominent American inventor and futurist. He got in touch with Kurzweil's agent, who told him that he hadn't been in contact with Kurzweil. All he knew was that he'd gone to work for Donald Trump at an undisclosed location.

Rothstein suspected Trump Island, having visited there years ago himself. He'd wanted to know what it felt like to hunt human beings for sport, but after killing several government interns, he realized that he simply didn't have a taste for it.

He'd returned to the island in order to find Kurzweil, but was greeted by Trump and several prominent members of ISIS upon arrival.

Rothstein knew he was screwed when they pointed their guns at him.

He held up his hands in surrender.

Some others in his entourage tried to run back their plane, only to be gunned down like dogs on the runway.

Trump just smiled at Rothstein and said, "Don't worry, we need you alive."

Next thing he knew, he'd been shot in the neck with a tranquilizer dart.

In his final moments of consciousness, Rothstein overheard Trump saying to the terrorist leaders, "Okay, let's make a deal. You'll have your Jew mole; you just have to get your boys to become sharks. I'll have Kurzweil fix them up, and then Putin will pick them up. Then we'll make this *loser* into our very own Trojan horse...."

When he finally came to, he looked up and saw a rather

haggard-looking face looking down at him.

"Hello, old friend," Kurzweil said to him. "I am sorry for this, but Trump is helping me fulfill the prophecy of Singularity, so I will never die. He has promised that I will be one of his chosen, so please, forgive me...."

"What... have you done, Ray...?" Rothstein mumbled in his stupor. He discovered that he'd been strapped to a gurney of some kind. "Oh God, dear Yahweh... please... help me...."

"God cannot, I'm afraid," Kurzweil continued. "The Singularity and its machinery have replaced God's will, and I have taken away yours. You are now part machine; you are a virus to infect the Jews. You will retain your own thoughts, but your heart and soul are henceforth controlled by the machine. Soon we will *all* become machines, but until then, you are a drone against Israel…whether you want to be or not."

Rothstein was allowed to leave the island only because he'd been programed to do so.

Whenever his former self would try to speak, the machine inside him would shut him down.

The machine had one directive for him—ensure the Prime Minster's reelection.

Using all of his charisma and intelligence, Rothstein stumped for Netanyahu in the months to come, and predictably he won in a landslide. The Prime Minister rewarded him with a cabinet position.

All was going according to plan.

The voices had kept quiet for most of the day, but now that the Prime Minister had left the room, they were telling him to put his finger on Netanyahu's security console.

TOUCH IT.

TOUCH IT NOW.

TOUCH IT NOW!!!

Heeding the voice in his head, Rothstein reached out and placed his finger on the computer screen.

When the Prime Minister returned, he thought it odd that Rothstein was touching his console, but he was even more surprised when the spectral image of Osama Bin Laden appeared on its screen.

The cabinet officials were aghast.

Rothstein kept his finger on the screen to broadcast the message as Bin Laden began to speak.

"Hello, disgusting Jew pigs," the deceased leader of Al-Qaeda warmly greeted them. "As you know, I have already passed. I am in Heaven right now with my 72 virgins, and yet—just like you secularists with your smartphones and facebooks—I live on within the *machine*. Up until now, you Jews have used your machines to keep the Muslim people down, but now we shall turn your own machines against you. You will lose your precious Internet as well as your defenses, and I will defeat you even in death. We have finally found a way to wipe your sickening race from this planet. Allah Hu Akbar."

Bin Laden's image disappeared and Rothstein drew his gun, but the Mossad commandos opened fire before he could use it. His body riddled with bullets, his consciousness briefly returned as he collapsed onto the floor.

"Forgive me, mother Israel," he coughed, blood dripping

from his mouth. "Yahweh, please forgive me...."

Rothstein may have found peace in death, but the implications of Bin Laden's message were anything but peaceful to the remaining cabinet members.

One of the Prime Minister's tech specialists ran over to the computer and tried operating it, but all that came up onscreen was a meme featuring Steve Jobs, a man revered by the Arabs for his Syrian heritage.

Steve Jobs was dressed as a sheik. His image bore the following text:

ISRAEL IS A VIRUS

THAT WILL NOW INFECT ITSELF

The tech specialist typed fast in his attempt to kill the virus, but the meme would not disappear. When a black dialogue box finally popped up, Netanyahu didn't know whether to feel relief or terror.

"What is it?" the Prime Minister demanded to know. "Tell me!"

"It says that the entirety of Israeli Internet has been compromised," the specialist replied. "But... that makes no sense! We're still online right now. Here, look."

The specialist then entered the URL for TMZ.com, and the following headline appeared:

CELEBS GONE MISSING, INCLUDING ENTIRE CAST OF SHARK TANK!

"See, it still works!" the Prime Minister cried in jubilation. It was then that he noticed the small ticker box at the lower right corner of the screen. "Wait, what is that?" he asked.

The specialist got down on his knees, as if he were about to pray.

"It… it is a *miracle*," he gasped. "I don't know how or why, but it seems we have been blessed with the Internet for another 8 hours, just like when God gave Israel light for 8 days.... Prime Minister, this is like the Hanukah of the Twenty-First Century! Yahweh has given us *time*. We might survive this after all!"

The Prime Minster looked at the clock and said, "I don't believe much in miracles or even God these days. We must prepare our defensive forces whether the Internet works or not! There are sharks coming, and their mission is to feast on our flesh."

Chapter 6

Trump Island

"This white woman's liver is *delicious*. I love white woman liver!" Museveni exclaimed, slowly savoring the internal organs of Katy Perry.

"Damn you!" Putin screamed in anger. "*I* wanted to kill Katy Perry and fuck her corpse straight! How *dare* she sing such a catchy tune about kissing girls!"

Meanwhile, Trump was busy torturing the fallen-from-grace quarterback, RG3. He'd had him strung up by his ankles from a nearby tree.

"I lost my fantasy league because of you," he sputtered while pissing in his face. "Such a loser, and I am not! I don't *ever* lose, and now you will pay, RG3."

Trump took the knife out RG3's thigh, reached down and slit his throat.

Hiding behind a nearby boulder, Aaron Rodgers could only look on in horror. Still, he'd known since RG3's first season that the kid was never going to make it.

Sitting behind him was Stephen Hawking, and crouching in the bushes behind them were Kobe Bryant and Jennifer Lawrence.

J-Law knew she needed to form a group of two alpha males and one smart nerd. The method actress had somehow found herself in a real-life version of the *Hunger Games*, and so she'd been forced to reprise her role as Katniss Everdeen one last time.

"Kobe," she whispered to the shooting guard who had his eyes set on Jinping. "We *have* to get Rodgers and Hawking for our team."

"What team, bitch?" Kobe whispered back. "I don't need any help. I'm hiding from that crazy-ass Trump, but you'd best believe I'm gonna kill that Chinese bastard before I let him out of my sight."

"Don't call me a bitch, asshole. I was in four *Hunger Games* movies and I've worked with Bradley Cooper not once but *twice*. I know how to survive. When they are gone, follow me. And don't get it twisted 'cause I'm not Shaq—I'm *Katniss*, motherfucker."

"A'ight'," Kobe said, "but I'm gonna kill that bitch-ass President Jinping...."

"Fine," Lawrence replied, "but to kill them all, first we must survive."

The four psychopathic leaders left their kills behind and

walked off to the west. Each of them was hoping to get the easy kill of Kevin Hart out of the way before nightfall.

"THEY ARE GONE, AARON RODGERS," came Steven Hawking's electronic voice from behind him. "WE MUST FIND THE OTHERS AND FORMULATE A STRATEGY FOR SURVIVAL."

Rodgers turned around and looked the genius scientist in his eyes.

"WE MUST FIND AT LEAST TWO STRONG TYPE A PERSONALITIES," Hawking continued, "TO INCREASE OUR CHANCES OF SURVIVAL FROM 27% TO 52.36%."

Rodgers nodded and said, "It's like going for two, I get it. You're the strategist, Coach. But who's gonna make us a better team? I haven't seen any of those *Shark Tank* or *Predator* people since we all scattered."

"Screw them," J-Law replied as Bryant and her stepped out of the bushes. "You guys are on our team, now."

"That's right, and y'all should be smiling with gratitude," Bryant said. "You just drafted the greatest baller of all time AND that *Hunger Games* bitch in one round."

"I told you not to call me that, fucker!" Lawrence said. "But it's true, I am one bad-ass fucking bitch. You should be grateful we found you; could've been Kevin Hart and Larry David instead."

"What the fuck, man!?" Kevin Hart squealed, tears flowing from his horrified eyes. He stood trembling beside a confused-looking Larry David. "I'm being hunted on a secret island by the Russian and Chinese Presidents, some tribal lord, and Donald Trump, and I got no weapons, no phone, no nothing. God help me! Help me, Lord! I never held it against you for making me so short and I *still* praised your name on Twitter. Please, Lord, don't let me die next to Larry fucking David!"

David wiped the sweat from his brow and said, "I realize now that I shouldn't have called Trump a racist on SNL. I shouldn't have done it, but eh, it's like a vacation, it's free. We get to see the sun, not bad. But you know what I've learned? There is something about rich guys with bad hair; they are very dangerous people. I knew one, not wealthy like Trump, but I told him he looked like he'd had an AIDS patient's pubic hair glued to his head, and this guy, a long-time friend, he *blocked* me on Facebook. People get too sensitive these days, but this weather, eh, not bad. If we gotta die, eh, not too shabby."

"Larry!" Hart squealed. "We *are* gonna die, man! You and me, we ain't no killers! We gonna *die*, man, and soon! I don't wanna die! I got so much left to live for...."

David just shrugged and held out his palms in his usual, eh-what-are-you-going-to-do manner. "Eh," he said, "better here than Brooklyn."

"Nigga, I *want* to be back in Brooklyn, or LA, or *anywhere* but here. I don't wanna die on Donald Trump Island. I wanna Christian burial, with my babies and famous people at my funeral. I want the *works*, man."

"Who's more famous than Trump?" countered David. "He'll be there to say goodbye, at least. That's somebody."

"Shut the fuck up, Larry!"

"No, you shut up," came a voice from behind them.

There stood a shirtless Putin, bow drawn on them both. With a blood-stained handkerchief tied around his head, he looked a bit like a Russian Rambo.

"Oh shit… aw man…" Hart whined, feces dripping from his cargo shorts. "I really did just shit myself. I'm gonna die with shit in my pants…"

He dropped to his knees and tried praying to God, but an arrow pierced his throat before he could even begin.

"Amen," Putin said for him. "You will make good fertilizer."

Larry David shrugged and said, "Personally, I couldn't kill a black guy; I'd feel too much guilt. I try to be nice to the blacks, you know, they've had it bad. Nice kid, but I never understood his popularity. Not a great comedian, he was no Chris Rock… but eh, what are you going to do. Listen Putin, before you kill me, can I make a death request?"

"What do you speak of, Jew?"

"I've had this bad crick in my neck, so could you please not shoot me, and maybe just snap it instead? If I'm gonna die, I wanna work this crick out before I go."

"You are a brave one, Jew. I watch your show on TV once. My ex-wife Lyudmila like it. Much better than *Everyone Loves Rumoney*. That man chump and non-male. You, you at least speak truth, even while deathly annoying. Admirable."

"My rabbi would get after me for not having a filter. I wish I could tell him the leader of Russia respects it. Could you at least email him what you said about me, after you kill me?"

"We will see, Jew. For now, I let you live. You will be my Jew dog and round up the others. If you do good job and we kill Trump, then maybe I make you court jester."

Larry David shrugged and said, "Eh, it can't be any worse than being in a Woody Allen movie."

Meanwhile, the actors from the *Predator* films and the cast of *Shark Tank* were wandering through the jungle. Both groups understood from their experience in the *Predator* films and making deals on *Shark Tank* that they'd have better odds working together than going it alone.

Reaching a stream, Kevin O'Leary and Arnold Schwarzenegger both knelt down to quench their thirst. While gulping water from his cupped hands, Schwarzenegger noticed the badly decomposed corpses just upstream.

Schwarzenegger leapt back and spat the water out, but O'Leary bravely swallowed it down. "The dead have minerals," he explained, "and we will need them to survive."

Down on all fours, Adrian Brody drank directly from the stream. "He's right," he said between laps. "When I had to bulk up for *Predators*, I drank water with human ashes in it. Drink this corpse water if you want to live."

Jesse Ventura, Carl Weathers, and Mark Cuban all joined Brody by the stream, but the remaining *Shark Tank* members, Barbara, Daymond, Robert, and Lori decided to stay put.

Robert, who was the nicest on the show, looked nauseous and said, "Look, we all have to work together and keep our humanity. We need to respect the dead. We can't live off of…" he dry heaved and continued, "…corpse water. We need to find food and work together so we can stop these twisted leaders from destroying the world!"

O'Leary wiped his chin and fished out a large femur from the bottom of the stream.

He went over to Robert and said, "We didn't have enough food before, but we do now!"

Barbara tried to defend him as O'Leary bashed in his skull, but he kicked her in the stomach, knocking her to the ground beside him. Both of them were beaten until their screams finally stopped, their bloodied bodies lying motionless beside the stream. O'Leary was happy knowing that their bones would provide future minerals for it.

Daymond shook his head and said, "I know you too well, Kevin. Ain't nothing wonderful about Mr. Wonderful, but I want you in my corner. I'm sorry, Lori," he continued, looking to his soon-to-be ex colleague, "but Kevin does things in three."

Lori was too busy sobbing over her dead friends, and before she could even ask what Daymond meant, O'Leary clubbed her on the back of the neck.

She collapsed onto Barbara and Robert, and O'Leary then proceeded to administer his most brutal beat-down yet, taking out all of his pent-up anger toward her for every deal she had ever taken from him on TV.

"I'm too old for this shit," Danny Glover mumbled, rising from his seat on a nearby stump. "I can't do this. I can't…."

And with that, he stumbled off into the jungle alone.

O'Leary held up his bloody bone club, addressing those who were still with him.

"The *Predator* films and *Shark Tank* are both truths of life," he declared. "*We* are the fit! Together, even without any real weapons, we can defeat these tyrants! Arnold, Carl, and you, conspiracy guy… you were a wrestler, right?"

Ventura just glowered at him in response.

"Hey, what about me?" Cuban protested.

"Mark, you're schmuck, but a smart schmuck, and I'm glad to have you on. With the *Predator/Shark Tank* alliance, I do believe that we can get off of this island alive!"

ACT 3

Chapter 7

Open Water: The Atlantic Ocean

Muammar Gaddafi and Condoleezza Rice stood together on the lower deck of the cruise ship. They held hands while looking out across the ocean. The song "Who Dat Girl" by Flo Rida was playing on the sound system, and Gaddafi was fondly reminiscing on his first encounter with the former Secretary of State.

The State Department had declared Gaddafi dead back in 2011, but they had found him hiding in a bunker after the Libyan revolution. Safely hidden away behind his Amazonian Guard and mountainous pallets of canned goods, he'd been passing the time writing poetry about an unknown African princess.

Deciding he was worth more to them alive than dead, the American forces took him and his guards to a military base in

Afghanistan. They knew he had connections to terrorists and wanted intel, but he wouldn't say a word.

Frustrations mounted, but eventually a young CIA agent found something they could use in his psychological profile. The agent had minored in poetry, and in analyzing his poems about the mysterious African princess, she determined that these were the only moments where Gaddafi showed any real care or concern for someone besides himself.

Many of her higher-ups thought that 'she' was just a symbol for the former colonies still being controlled by Western imperial forces, but this poetry-reading agent formulated the theory that 'she' was actually in reference to Condoleezza Rice.

The State Department had records of Gaddafi making sexual comments regarding Secretary Rice in the past, but they'd assumed these were a form of power posturing and nothing more. In comparing her State Department transcripts to his poems, the young agent argued that Gaddafi's statements on then-Secretary Rice were in fact the only genuine things he had ever told the United States.

The State Department and President Obama agreed to test the young agent's thesis, seeing if they could use it to finally get some leverage on the recalcitrant Gaddafi. Coming out of retirement to help, Condoleezza Rice reluctantly agreed to use her feminine charms in any way she could if it would help them win the war on terror.

The CIA asked Gaddafi if he would be willing to work individually with former Secretary of State Rice, and he agreed.

Going into their interrogations, Rice expected the job to be a hard one, but she certainly didn't expect to fall in love.

Gaddafi had a rough exterior but a beautiful violent spirit, exhibiting the same passion she'd felt back when she was first learning to play the piano. Whenever they'd lock eyes across the table, the notes of her favorite Classical piece, Mozart's Concerto in D Minor, would begin to play in her head.

There was clearly something between them, but Rice did her best to keep things professional. She tried very hard to keep their discussions centered on terrorism, but more and more they just wound up flirting.

The song in her head was getting louder, and he was wearing her down.

On their tenth weekly session, she finally blocked the cameras, dropped her panties, and spread her legs for him.

While she expected that a man who kept concubines would know how to please a woman, she was surprised by Gaddafi's skills in making love. His fat Arabian cock filled her up just right, and the way he touched her with his lips and fingertips, he made her feel like a perfectly tuned piano.

They began having daily interrogation sessions after that.

Their post-coital discussions were often just as enjoyable as the sex. The two of them talked about life, love, and even American pop culture. Rice joked that their relationship reminded her of her two favorite shows on TV, *Homeland* and *Blacklist*.

Those moments of love felt like ages ago as they stood upon the deck of T-Pain's cruise ship.

Gaddafi's nostalgia-filled heart felt as heavy as the RPG-7 strapped to his back. He looked out across the waves with his

African princess, Condoleezza. The hard and pounding motion of the ocean reminded them both of those passionate nights together, but their blissful reverie wouldn't last long.

"Oh my fucking God!" Rice screamed, pointing out over the railing.

Gaddafi had never heard his love curse like that before, even in the throes of passion. Looking down, he saw what had alarmed her.

Sharks. Four of them. Swimming up along their starboard side.

Only these weren't any ordinary sharks. From the look of their grotesquely malformed bodies, they were human beings molded and morphed into the bodies of great white sharks. They were a science project gone wrong with the faces and personalities of their former human selves.

Staring in disbelief, Rice was able to recognize some of the Tibetan monks from the CIA target list, and Gaddafi knew the porn stars on sight. He enjoyed Bonnie Rotten for her oral skills, Alexis Texas for her anal, and James Deen for his brutal cock pounding, although he was currently unaware of the latter's pending rape charges.

James Deen was the first Singularity shark to jump out of the water and attack the ship. Like his former human self, it also sported a large, pendulous erection. It used its big shark dick to hump a hole in the hull before lumbering up over the railing and onto the deck.

The female porn sharks followed close behind. Using the shark teeth protruding from their erect nipples and clits, they scaled the side of the ship with ease.

Last was the three-headed monk shark, tortured by its unnatural existence. Six eyes stared up at their prey with equal parts horror and hunger. The animalism of the shark inside was ready to feed, but their human voices begged in robotic monotone, "PLEASE, KILL US."

Letting go of his lover's hand, Gaddafi unslung his grenade launcher without a second thought. He pulled the trigger and freed the monk's souls from Singularity sharkdom with one glorious blast.

The monks thanked Dharma to leave this life, but unfortunately Gaddafi was wasn't quick enough to reload.

He screamed in fury as the James Deen shark rammed its drill dick right through Rice's back, squirting its cum along with her blood through the gaping hole in her chest. While Gaddafi struggled to load another grenade, it came after him with her lifeless corpse still bobbing from its monster cock like a puppet. Nearly ten feet in length, the thick purple appendage pulsated with shark semen as it twisted through the air toward him.

"DIE, motherfucker!" Gaddafi cried, slamming the grenade round home. With a *WHOOSH* and a *BLAM*, the James Deen shark suddenly found itself with half a dick. Its brain completely obliterated, the hulking brute of a man-shark fell to the deck with a deafening crash.

Gaddafi's victory was to be short-lived, however, as the Bonnie Rotten shark bit him in half from behind. She didn't get to enjoy the meal, though, as his self-destruct implants detonated in her mouth. In all her years of doing porn, she had never taken such a power load.

Shark, man, and woman flesh rained down upon the last shark left, Alexis Texas.

She may have been a Shark of Singularity like the others, but she still had the desires of a human nymphomaniac. Sensing the powerful pheromones of Bill Clinton nearby, she set off in search of her old flame.

*** Featuring special guest writer, Mandy De Sandra ***

While his wife was putting together a think tank on the top deck of the ship, Bill Clinton snuck off with a young hipster girl from Buzzfeed. Her name was Tiffany and Bill Clinton was her first crush and realization that she was attracted to older men with power.

When Tiffany was seven, she not only had a crush on Bill Clinton, but she'd even made lists of what she loved the most about him. From his nice thumb to his sexy voice, she listed all of her favorite qualities.

These lists gave Tiffany a sense of happiness that homework

and real boys could not. She started looking for other famous men of power, making lists of their best qualities as well.

Tiffany's parents were less than enthused by this hobby of hers. For the next ten years, they found her salacious lists all over the house.

Her mother had finally had enough. "Tiffany," she told her daughter over dinner, "you bombed your SATs because all you do is make lists of then top ten things about hot rich famous guys you'll never even meet. You keep this up and you are never going to able to find a job, and you will always have to rely on a man who is not rich or famous."

"Whatever mom," Tiffany scoffed, "I am going to become a writer for Buzzfeed and a fourth-wave feminist. I'll get what I want and do what I want!"

Her mother had laughed at her then, but Tiffany was getting the last laugh now.

She had become senior staff writer of listicles for Buzzfeed, and now she was unlocking her cabin door to invite former President Bill Clinton inside.

Bill Clinton closed the door behind them and went straight for the bottle of scotch on the shelf. Pouring them both a drink, he handed her a glass and said, "Tiffany, it warms my heart to meet such a lifelong fan."

They clinked glasses and took a sip of scotch. He then set his glass down on the table and gave a Tiffany an enthusiastic thumbs up. "This scotch is aged nice and smooth," he said with a wry smile. "It's almost like drinking myself."

Tiffany laughed and said, "I still have my first list about you memorized. It was you who inspired me to pursue my passion for listicles."

"Honey, speaking of," Clinton said as he leaned in close, "I don't suppose you have any *popsicles* in here? Some raspberry ones would be great."

"I have a raspberry right here," she said, lifting up her dress to show she wasn't wearing panties.

Clinton looked at her dark pink lips and said, "I really wanted a popsicle, but young pussy is just as refreshing. Come here, darling."

"Ooooh, this is like a fantasy come true! Take me, President Clint–AHHHHH!!!"

The Alexis Texas shark burst through the floorboards and devoured Tiffany from the waist down. Her upper half landed on the nearby bunk, horrified eyes meeting the porn shark's predatory glare.

Alexis Texas nuzzled her snout against Tiffany's perky C-cups and said, "IT'S A SHAME, THOSE ARE SOME NICE REAL TITS." She then bit them off, as if they were after-dinner mints to cleanse her pallet.

Clinton was surprised to find himself sexually excited by the gory scene.

Looking deep into the eyes of the porn shark, he recognized her instantly. He remembered those very same eyes looking up at him in the midst of some frenzied, coke-fueled fellatio, sometime back in the mid-2000s. Bill had hooked up with many random women over the course of his illustrious life, but Alexis Texas was the best sex he'd ever had.

"Well I'll be," he said, reaching out to tenderly stroke her gills, "I know those eyes better than my own momma's chili, Alexis Texas. Honey, even when they turn you into a shark, you're still beautiful. Still, whoever did this must be a mad man. To cut that human booty of yours was a crime against humanity."

"DONALD TRUMP INVITED ME TO A PARTY," she replied, the sadness evident in her robotic shark voice. "BUT IT WASN'T A PARTY. THERE WASN'T EVEN ANY GOOD COKE THERE, JUST SOME WEIRD-ASS MACHINE AND A BUNCH OF BIG WATER TANKS. HE HAD SOME GUY NAMED RAY TURN ME, JAMES, AND BONNIE INTO HUMANOID CYBER-SHARKS!!!"

"That son of a gun," Clinton said, "I told Hillary you can't trust a man with good money but bad hair. You learn these truths in politics, beautiful."

The porn shark began wagging her big, voluptuous tail fin with sexual heat. "THERE ARE MACHINES INSIDE OF ME, BILL." she said. "NOT LIKE VIBRATING BEADS OR STUFF THAT FEELS GOOD, THOUGH. SOMETHING... ELSE. SOMETHING THAT DISTORTS EVERYTHING MY NINTH GRADE SCIENCE TEACHER WHO I FUCKED EVER TAUGHT ME. I JUST FEEL SO MUCH DESIRE FOR BLOOD, LIKE THAT TWILIGHT GUY WITH THE SEXY HAIR...."

"I loved that movie, a beautiful tale about love, faith, and baseball," Clinton replied. "But that sounds terrible, my dear."

"THEY PROGRAMMED US TO EAT ANYTHING IN THE VICINITY OF THE PRESIDENT AND THE

DIRECTOR OF THE NSA. I WANT TO FEED, I NEED TO FEED, AND YET THE HUMAN PART OF ME, THE PART THAT MADE ME THE TOP ANAL STAR OF THE DECADE—IT NEEDS TO FUCK YOU, MR. PRESIDENT. RIGHT NOW. PLEASE FUCK ME NOW, OR I SWEAR I WILL EAT YOU AND EVERY LAST MOTHERFUCKER ON THIS MOTHERFUCKING SHIP!!!"

"Well, I never fucked a shark before," he said, giving her his signature sincere-but-not-sincere look, "but I have enjoyed some big girls down in Arkansas."

The Texas shark's vagina pulsated with the power of the ocean.

The human part of her remembered the pleasure of Bill's big dick. After fucking and cumming hard with Bill, Alexis often thought it such a shame that he'd gone into politics instead of porn. If there really was a Heaven up there, she didn't want to go unless it involved fucking Bill Clinton.

She was still unsure of how his cock would feel inside her now, but she was ready to find out.

"I guess we won't need a condom this time," Clinton said. "So that's a plus. I do love me some raw shark sashimi, but this will be even better."

"TAKE ME, BILL!" she cried, flopping down onto the floor and spreading her big fat shark cunt using her pectoral fins. "LET ME FEEL MORE HUMAN THAN SHARK AGAIN, JUST ONE LAST TIME! I NEED THAT COCK, BIG BUBBA. PLEASE, PLEEEEAASE GIVE IT TO ME AND GIVE IT TO ME GOOD!!!"

Bill fingered her large, wet pussy from behind. "It feels good and ready. I haven't had one this loose since that girl from *Teen Mom*, but I do like a challenge."

Clinton dropped his pants and mounted her. He stuck his cock all the way in and Alexis moaned with pleasure. With vocal chords that were part human and part shark, she emitted an unearthly shriek that sounded like a banshee underwater.

It turned Bill on, and he fucked her even harder.

Flipping her over onto her back, he stuck his face between her big shark tits and looked up to see her razor-toothed smile. It was primal and scary and a huge turn on to be fucking a creature who could kill him at any moment.

"YES, YES, YEEEESSSSSSS!!!" she screamed and squirted hard.

It was as big as a wave, shark pussy juice coating Clinton and splattering the walls of the cabin. The added lubrication produced a tingling sense of euphoria on Clinton's naked skin, causing him to ejaculate immediately.

He had never came so hard before in his entire life—it almost felt like he'd shot his whole dick off inside of her.

Wiping the sweat and squirt from his tingling face, he was

horrified to find his skin melting off in his hand. In a sudden panic, he tried to pull his melting cock out of the shark's vagina, but he'd been hooked in tight.

"OH SHIT..." Alexis said. "THE MACHINE INSIDE ME, IT'S TAKING YOUR CONSIOUSNESS AND CUM AND MAKING US AS ONE.... OH SHIT... I'M SORRY, BILL... I WAS... SENT HERE... TO DO THIS... TO YOU...."

Starting with his pelvic area, Clinton could feel more and more of his body morphing into the Texas shark. He had read about Singularity theory and liked the idea of becoming an immortal sex-machine, but he never thought the opportunity would arise in his lifetime. He'd also wondered whether it would hurt to die and lose his old body, but he found that there was very little pain involved. Just that sweet, tingling sensation, like his whole entire being was being stimulated onto a higher plane of existence.

After his body had been absorbed into hers, his mind melded with her shark brain as well. As he slowly sat up and looked in the mirror across the room, he saw a shark with his facial structure staring back at him.

A face that showed the hunger in its eyes, an imminent need to feed.

MD <3

Admiral Rogers, Hillary Clinton, and DMX all stood behind T-Pain, who was currently manning the ship. T-Pain wasn't an official Captain or even licensed to drive a cruise ship, but the other Miami rappers onboard had given him the job based on his experience in the music video, "I'm On A Boat."

Rogers could tell that T-Pain didn't even know which direction was east, let alone how to follow coordinates to any secret island. "Son," he said, "I enjoyed that comical song with you and that weird-looking kid from SNL just as much as the next guy, but I'm a Navy man, so I'll be manning the ship now. Epstein here will be my First Mate. He's the only one who even knows where the hell this island is."

"See, Hillary," Epstein said with smirk. "I shouldn't be locked up; I'm proving myself useful after all!"

"Fine with me," T-Pain said as he turned to face Hillary. "How 'bout it, Clint? You wanna grab some syrup and be my wing for all these lil' white-girl, list-makin' hoes?"

Under normal circumstances, Hillary would have given him a speech on why the term 'hoe' was not only sexist but also racist against migrant farm workers, but there was no time for talk.

"Mr. Pain," she said, "I have a world to save and an island

to reach. Donald Trump has nukes out there and *we* have to stop him. Our sex lives can wait."

"Yo, half these hoes have already been up in The Don's shit. They probably got some info, just talk to them about national security while I spit some game. When the stakes are high, the panties get low."

Hillary pondered this for a moment. The kids from Buzzfeed might actually have intel on Trump Island that the even the Admiral and the NSA hadn't been able to get ahold of.

"Okay, Mr. Pain," she said, "I shall accompany you as your 'wing', but it is not to help you with the 'hoes', as you call them. This is truly a matter of national security."

"Word Clint, it's all good, cause I'm good at spotting haters and snakes…" he said, and then began to sing, "Haters and snakes / playing patty cake / niggaz hanging wit da president / of the muthafuckin' United States."

"That's enough, Mr. Pain." Hillary said, looking down at the pool from the wheelhouse. It was still filled with drunken young people, and there was a large banner draped above it.

BUZZFEED: THE NEW NEWS, it read.

Most of the twenty- and thirty-something's were busy partying hard, but there was one solitary man drinking by himself at a table off to the side. Hillary recognized him as the anti-feminist Gamergate journalist, Milo Yiannopoulos, popularly known as Nero.

"What the hell is *that* asshole doing here?" Hillary asked. "Come with me, Mr. Pain, I think we could have a spy on this boat who is also a terrible human being."

T-Pain followed Hillary down the stairs that lead to the open pool deck.

Walking straight up to Nero's table, Hillary said, "I don't know what the hell you are doing here you misogynist bastard, but you won't be staying on this ship any longer. This is a matter of national security, and I know you are working with Trump."

"Bloody Christ..." Nero said and finished his drink. "I don't even want to be here," he continued, throwing his empty glass overboard, "not with all these beta males and basic-ass bitches. If I hear about another fucking list or some stupid social justice crusade, I swear to God I'm gonna fucking kill somebody."

"Why *are* you here then, Nero?"

He just shook his head and replied, "I lost a bloody bet to Gavin McInnes. I'll bet that sexy stud is still laughing about me being stuck on this lame-ass ship. So, Hillary, with all due respect, why don't do something constructive, loosen the fuck up, and go let your husband fuck you in the ass."

"I'D RATHER EAT YOUR CANDY ASS, SON," came a mechanical voice from behind him. The list-makers all turned and screamed at what they saw.

Hillary gasped and watched in horror as a shark resembling her husband tackled Nero to the deck. Before he even knew what hit him, the Clinton/Texas shark had corkscrewed its big shark dick right up the kid's ass.

"Oooooh!" Nero cried in reaction to the surprise anal assault.

"Oh my god, no!" Hillary screamed. "Not my husband, no!"

Having completely skewered Nero by that point, the Clinton/Texas shark held him up like a shish kabob and devoured him in one bite, sucking the man's flesh right off of its own shark cock.

"IT WASN'T GAY, HONEY," the Clinton/Texas shark explained. "SEE, I AM ALSO PART WOMAN. ALEXIS TEXAS IS SHARING THIS BODY WITH ME. BUT YOU KNOW WHAT BUTTERCUP, I FEEL CONNECTED TO ALL THE SHARKS IN ALL THE LANDS. I CAN FEEL MY SHARK BROTHERS AND SISTERS SWIMMNING ALL THROUGHOUT THE MIDDLE EAST, AND LIKE ME THEY ARE READY TO FEED… OHHH, I CAN FEEEEL THE OTHERS INSIDE OF ME NOW.…

The Clinton/Texas shark doubled over writhing in pain, like it was about to lose control of its bowels. "IT'S NOT SHARK POOP THAT'S COMING," it wailed at the horrified audience, "OHHHH, I THINK I'M HAVING BABIES.…"

Chapter 8

ISIS On Instagram

Only a small minority of ISIS members were allowed to become Sharks of Singularity. Those select few chosen typically came from two very different backgrounds: young affluent Muslims from oil-rich countries, or those from Europe who felt existential angst.

Both types were shipped off to Trump Island to become sharks, but the vast majority of ISIS soldiers were left behind to wage holy war and secure the shark-ravaged territories for their new Islamic state. Their goal was to unite all nations under Mohammed's rule, starting with the Holy Land.

There were a few members of ISIS who weren't cut out to be sharks or jihadists, but their leader, Bakr al-Baghdadi, had said that all men would have a purpose in Jihad. These men were more artists than fighters. They didn't exactly make for great marksmen or suicide bombers, but could take a good picture or deliver a good joke.

Bakr had decided that these men, cursed as they were with weak-minded Western attributes, could still serve some purpose in the great Jihad. By harnessing their technological savvy and artistic aptitudes, they could help keep up morale, sharing their photos and jokes on social media.

Their great and wise Caliph saw that not only could social media be used to coordinate attacks and attract new recruits, it could also be used to show off their grand accomplishments in the Final Holy Battle, much like Westerners used it to show off what they ate for lunch each day.

For the men in the trenches and those guarding home base, they could all feel connected by the images of their brothers in action, entertained by the ISIS Sharks of Singularity.

On the official ISIS Instagram page, there were daily updates from around the world. The most popular photo of late had been taken during the ISIS shark attack on Mecca.

<u>Photo 1</u>

Location: Mecca, Saudi Arabia

In the foreground, a man kneels in prayer before the Ka'ba, but the focus is on the shark in the background, lunging toward him with its jaws open wide. The photo includes the following caption:

We have cleansed the holiest of holy lands. All "Muslims" who have not joined ISIS are not true Muslims. God's sharks shall punish the infidels with His divine wrath. Allah Hu Akbar! #MondayMotivation #GodIsGreat #Blessed #TheFinalJihad

<u>Photo 2</u>

Location: Dubai, The United Arab Emirates

In a luxurious shopping mall in the heart of Dubai, there are shoppers being attacked by ISIS sharks. Vacationing Americans are screaming down the indoor ski slope as ISIS sharks chase them down. One fat man with his back to the slopes, enjoying some cotton candy, is about to be bitten in half. On the other side of the slopes, ISIS sharks chase women through a Victoria's Secret. A shark with a pink thong dangling from its fin is heading straight for the food court.

Real Muslims don't ski! The United Arab Emirates is the most decadent and westernized of Arab nations, and soon they shall be shark food. #ISISHitsTheSlopes #VictoriasSecretIsOut #SharkFood #TheFinalJihad

<u>Photo 3</u>

Location: Lalibela, Ethiopia

In the dry lands of an Ethiopian village, a poor and hungry Christian boy is being chased by an ISIS sand shark, kicking up dust and screaming as he runs for his life. Other behind him are being eaten and dragged away. An ISIS shark and a lion are fighting over the body of a deceased tribal leader.

The infidels are starving for Allah, but our shark brothers of ISIS enjoy a light snack before continuing Jihad. #EthiopianDiet #TheFinalJihad #NoOneIsSafe #InfidelToOrder

<u>Photo 4</u>

Location: Cairo, Egypt

In Cairo, tourists and citizens alike are screaming in horror, shark fins circling the sand around the pyramids. The infidels are desperately trying to climb up the pyramids, bloody and splattered with gore. The Great Pyramid of Giza itself is shown halfway sunken and sideways, human carnage littering the sand all around it.

The landmarks of the Jahiliyyah shall perish along with them. #InfidelsBeLike #ISISGoesHard #Armageddon #WalkLikeAnEgyptianToHell

<u>Photo 5</u>

Location: Raqqa, Syria

ISIS home base. A USO-type show for ISIS is currently taking place. There is a huge crowd of ISIS soldiers watching a five-man a cappella group onstage, performing in matching black robes. Known as The Beheaded Baritones, they are singing while several homosexuals are about to be executed. The executioner holds up his sword and gives a big thumbs up before hacking off a hooded head.

Fun times at our variety show for the faithful. We have our favorite singers, The Beheaded Baritones, singing number-one ISIS hit "Heads Will Roll" before killing some homosexuals. They are only first batch, as the next will be stoned to death. #GoodTimes #ISISGoesHard #PartyLikeARockStar

<u>Photo 6 (#3 best joke)</u>

Location: Raqqa, Syria

At the same ISIS variety show, the main event, Jihad Jerry, stands center stage. The comedian stares out into the smiling crowd, looking like a deranged Bob Hope. In this one, the crowd is roaring with laughter as he discusses the previous executions.

What did the homosexual say at his beheading? That is not what I meant when I said I want to give you head. #1ISISComedian #FunnierThanTheJews #HeadsWillRoll #ISISVarietyShow

<u>Photo 7 (#2 best joke)</u>

Location: Raqqa, Syria

The ISIS variety show is a roaring success. The entire audience is smiling and laughing with glee. Jihad Jerry has a grotesque caricature of a Jewish banker doll onstage. Others in the crowd have similar dolls, holding them up by nooses.

How do you tell a Jew from a demon? The demon only tries to steal your soul to keep; the Jew steals your soul but then turns around and sells it for money. #NumberOneISISComedian #TheOnlyFunnyJewIsADeadOne #HeadsRollingLaughter #ISISVarietyShow

<u>Photo 8 (#1 best joke)</u>

Location: Raqqa, Syria

There is a group of five women bound onstage, covered head to toe in burkas. The only body parts visible are their eyes, from which tears are streaming. The men in the audience are wielding rocks the size of footballs in their hands. Jihad Jerry is pointing at the women and laughing.

What did the good-hearted ISIS member say to his wife who was raped? Honey, I'll only stone you on your bad side. #NumberOneISISComedian #PurityBall #ISISVarietyShow

<u>Photo 9 (ISIS profile pic)</u>

Location: Instagram

Front and center on the ISIS Instagram profile page, there is a poorly Photoshopped picture of ISIS sharks devouring various famous Jews: Netanyahu, Adam Sandler, Bernie Sanders, and Larry David.

Whether it be the leader of Israel or the creator of Seinfeld, all Jews will feel the wrath of Allah. We are coming and there is nowhere you can hide! #Jews4Jaws #ISISSharksOfSingularity #TheFinalJihad #LarryDavidWillDie

Chapter 9

Trump Island, Brunch Bungalow

"Pretty, pretty good. This is a pretty, pretty good brunch," Larry David told his captors, Trump, Putin, and Omarosa. "If I'm going to die, at least I'll have this in my stomach. Delicious, Mr. Trump. A cream cheese and pastrami omelet. Brilliant. I really believe psychopaths provide the best food; it's good people who make bad meals. They care too much. Psychopaths just want the best. You learn these things working in TV. Still, I never thought I'd experience a meal this good. It's even better than Katz's Deli. I swear to you, I could die a happy man right now."

David sipped his coffee obnoxiously, looking around the table at his fellow brunchers. For a man who didn't laugh all that often, Putin was certainly entertained by David, but neither Trump nor

Omarosa were amused by his comments.

The Nukes of Singularity slumbered in the bungalow behind them. Their bearded faces looked peaceful, and Trump was enjoying their silence. Some days during brunch they would go into their daily prayer routine out of habit. Trump didn't care for these interruptions, but he loved the power he felt eating near nuclear weapons, whether they spoke or not.

"These eggs are just fantastic," David reiterated, eyeing the sleeping sentient nukes. "I wonder if there would be any good side effects to nuclear weapons, like maybe radiation makes food taste better."

Putin just laughed and said, "This is Jew is so annoying, it makes me laugh so much. He is truly court jester for great man like me."

Trump looked displeased. "It is very distasteful," he began, "to make the *prey* an honorary brunch guest on Trump Island, Vladimir."

"Oh Trump, relax," David countered. "I should get one last good meal. You gotta at least respect *Seinfeld*, right?"

"No, that was a show for losers and about losers."

David just shrugged and continued eating.

"I like the Seinfeld," Putin said. "Having the Larry David around is like my own private Seinfeld show. Very good."

"Thank you Putin, I appreciate that," David said, glancing back at the ISIS Nukes of Singularity. "Before you guys kill me, can you let me fire at least one nuke? I've always wanted to kill a lot of people. You really can't admit that to anybody these days, but with you guys, I feel like I can be myself."

"How is it that you know so much about our plans, Jew?" Putin asked, no longer amused.

David just shrugged and said, "If you got a bunch of nukes, I figured you'd be planning on using them. Personally, I'd just live here and eat these omelets every day. I've never had anything so delicious."

"Enough of this nonsense," Trump said. "You're a loser who doesn't belong at this table. At brunch, the only rule is you respect the bungalow!"

"Don't harm him," Putin said. "I caught him. He is mine. He's my jester slave."

"I'm killing him," Trump said, "and if you try to stop me, I'll kill you too. My house, my rules!"

With that, Trump lunged across the table with a knife, but Putin only smiled and pressed a button on his cufflink. A hooked chain shot out from behind his back and smacked Trump on the wrist, sending his weapon clattering to the floor.

Trump rubbed his smarting hand, looking on in shock as more hooked chains rose up from behind Putin's back, hovering in the air like metallic snakes ready to strike.

They reminded Larry David of Doctor Octopus, or those brutal scenes from the *Hellraiser* movies.

Before either man could escalate the situation further, a computerized female voice interrupted their standoff. "INTRUDERS APPROACHING NEAR BUNGALOW, GAME APPROACHING," it said.

The men looked away from each other and up at the TV screen, which had switched to show the island's CCTV feeds.

One of them had spotted the *Shark Tank*/*Predator* alliance, slowly stalking toward the brunch bungalow.

"I was always going to win," Putin said to Trump. "I am bringer of pain. Russian scientists make me more powerful than Cenobite, more than man with pins in head. You cannot compete with me, Trump. I am Leviathan, and the world is mine to bring suffering."

"I thought that might've been a *Hellraiser* thing," Larry David said and shrugged. "Eh, I didn't care for that movie."

Trump just smiled and replied, "Oh, but I can compete and I *will* win, Putin. Because *I* have Ray Kurzweil...."

"We should have taken up brunch with Trump," Museveni said, his stomach rumbling as he trudged through the brush alongside Jinping. "In Uganda, we are always hungry. Maybe Mr. Trump would have let me chop off Omarosa's genitals, and we could have had fried clitoris. African clitoris is delicious. Very good in protein."

"Food?" Jinping responded, shaking Danny Glover's decapitated head at him from the end of his walking stick. "All you Africans ever think about is food! We Chinese just eat fish and do math. That is why *we* superpower, while Africans have elephants for cars."

"Don't knock elephants," Museveni said. "When I was a boy, I would inspect the villages for homosexuals. I rode elephant to each village. It was very strong and full of God's love. I train them to trample over all the gays."

"Fine, we can eat J-Law after I kill her."

"Well, here's your chance, motherfucker!" someone yelled from behind them.

The Ugandan President drew his machete and said, "White woman clitoris will have to do," before charging into the bushes.

"No, Museveni!" Jinping cried. "It is trap!"

BOOM!!!

The Ugandan President was decimated by a makeshift explosive device, reducing him to a puff of red mist.

"NOW," cried Stephen Hawking, roll-charging the Chinese President from the bushes. Then came Kobe Bryant from behind, Aaron Rodgers and J-Law flanking him from either side.

"DIE, JINPING," Hawking said, manipulating his mouth controls to launch a stake of sharpened metal at him. Fired from an improvised pipe cannon mounted on the back of his wheelchair, the stake had been aimed at Jinping's heart, but somehow it just stopped in midair.

Kobe Bryant tossed a large rock at Jinping's head like he was attempting a jump shot, but before it could cave in his skull, the boulder inexplicably shattered.

"Hahaha, American fools...." Jinping sneered.

Pointing his palm at the oncoming Hawking, he then lifted his arm and the wheelchair along with it, leaving the astrophysicist suspended in mid-air.

"No fucking way!" J-Law screamed. "How the fuck did you pull a Magneto?!"

Jinping flashed a cocky grin. "I'd heard Putin had harnessed powers of *Hellraiser*, so I have my scientists harness powers of *X-Men*. Like weather before, I now control *metal*. All the cool dictators are giving themselves powers these days, hahahahaha!"

Lifting both arms high above his head, Jinping contracted the magnetic field by closing his fists tight.

"OH FUCK" were Hawking's last words, before being crushed to death in his chair.

Pointing his hands at Rodgers and Bryant next, Jinping manipulated the metal eyelets in their shoes and the championship rings on their fingers, forcing them to fly at each other like that scene from *Crouching Tiger, Hidden Dragon*.

"You'll never get away with this, Jinping!" Rodgers yelled as he ducked one of Bryant's kicks.

"That's right, bitch!" Bryant hollered, narrowly dodging a flurry of Rodgers' fists.

Jinping watched with glee as the two top athletes wore themselves out, gradually losing their power to resist. Soon they were moving like zombies, sluggishly flailing their limbs at each other.

Growing bored, Jinping decided to finish them off, forcing the men to strangle each other until their both keeled over, clutching each other's throats on the jungle floor.

Standing there in the middle of the clearing, frozen with shock, it suddenly dawned on Jennifer Lawrence that she was the only one left. It was a very meta moment for her, realizing that even off-set, she still couldn't escape Magneto's power.

"I am going to win this competition, J-Law," the Chinese President told her. "China always win. I will be head of group and rule this world, but first, I have my fun with you, Miss Everdeen.... You have always been my fantasy girl, did you not know? I *big* fan of yours...."

"Fucking gross!" J-Law spat back.

"Hahaha, I fap to *all* your movies," Jinping continued. "Why, it was me behind the Fappening, you know. I had help from mole in NSA, but now, I have real thing! *Come* to Jinping, whore...."

He lifted his hand to draw her near, but somehow his powers of magnetism were no longer working. There came a loud *BEEEEEEP* and a puff of acrid smoke from behind his back.

"Made in China, huh, motherfucker," J-Law laughed. "Well, you can always count on a good old-fashioned American ass-whooping!"

She charged at him as Jinping screamed, "Fuck! NOOOO!!! My Magneto device is about to EXPLOOOO—"

KABLAAAM!!!

Before she could rip out his throat, J-Law perished in the same explosion, but she went in peace knowing she had finally punished The Fappener.

The *Predator/Shark Tank* alliance were the only captures left alive besides Larry David.

Kevin O'Leary led the group toward the bungalow and said, "We gotta hit them where they least expect it. I've read all of Trump's business books, and the guy doesn't miss brunch. Knowing him, they're dining in that bungalow as we speak."

"How do you know this? We've got to find a way off this planet!" Adrian Brody said, method acting like he was in *Predators* again.

"We are on Earth, Brody," O'Leary said, "and I know this because that is where I would have brunch with my competitors."

"It's true," Mark Cuban said. "I'd do the same."

"We gotta sneak attack," Jesse Ventura said, crouching in the tall grass. "Carl, Arnold. We gotta do this like we were back in the jungles on the *Predator* set."

"Trump and Putin must be terminated," Schwarzenegger agreed.

"I hope they're taping this for a *Predator* sequel..." Carl Weathers sighed.

"Follow me, guys," O'Leary said. "I see a satellite dish through the trees up ahead, and knowing Trump, he'd want to watch Fox Business News during brunch."

The group pressed forward, stalking through the jungle.

"We should have just let him on *Shark Tank*, Kevin," Cuban said. "We should have just let him do the fucking show...."

"I'd rather die than let that son of a bitch on *Shark Tank*," O'Leary replied.

"Did he buy and sell one of your favorite prostitutes, too?" Schwarzenegger asked.

"Worse, Arnie, much worse."

"He cook you a bad hamburger stew?" Weathers asked.

"*Much* worse."

"Well, what the hell did the guy do to you?" Ventura asked.

"Alright, you guys really wanna know?" O'Leary said. "I was supposed to be his fifth partner out here. It was supposed to be the Fantastic Five with me, him, Putin, Jinping, and Museveni, but that fucker cut me out of the deal. Instead of being one of the hunters, now I'm one of the hunted! I wanted to rule the world, too. Hell, it was my idea to do the sharks! Hello, *Shark Tank*? It all came from me, hello, branding, and now I'm just going to—"

"Die!" Schwarzenegger finished for him, snapping O'Leary's neck from behind.

The group of survivors stared aghast as O'Leary's corpse collapsed to the ground.

"He was just as bad as the men in there," Schwarzenegger explained, pointing to the bungalow. "Now, we must terminate them as well…"

"I never really liked the guy anyway," Cuban said, looking down at O'Leary's body, lying motionless in the sand. "He always stole my deals."

"Fuck it," Brody said, acting brave. "Let's go in there and show these motherfuckers who the *real* predators are!"

"These guys think they're the Illuminati," Ventura said, "but I'll show *them* the light—with my fists!"

"Come on!" Schwarzenegger said, taking off just as fast as his sixty-seven-year-old legs would carry him.

Getting closer now, they could hear Trump and Putin inside the bungalow. The *Shark Tank/Predator* alliance knew that this would be their only chance to take their captors by surprise, killing them quickly, but they failed to anticipate the chained hooks that suddenly came flying from around the corner.

Hooks that were sharper than shark teeth.

ACT 4

Chapter 10

Cruise Ship

Hungry newborn babies poured out of the Bill Clinton/ Alexis Texas shark's vaginal canal in a bloody torrent. They all had Alexis' breasts, Bill's face, and were about the size of human adults, but their appetites were even larger than their father/ mother combined.

As the Clinton/Texas shark continued popping out babies, it grew even hungrier still, longing to feed again. The act of continual birth only seemed to make it more ravenous, drooling in anticipation as its newborns began devouring all the delicious Buzzfeeders.

Two of them had gotten ahold of Pitbull, playing tug-of-war with his corpse.

"Clint! Duck n' run, girl!" DMX hollered at the President, aiming his bazooka at the Clinton/Texas Shark of Singularity. "Big Willy, you's my dog n' all, but you gotta go. Motherfuckin' sharks gotta the bite bullet, nah mean?"

Hillary ran back up to the wheelhouse and DMX prepared to fire.

"SAVE ME, BABY SHARKS!!!" the Clinton/Texas shark bellowed. "SAAAAVE MEEEEEEEEE!!!"

Abruptly ceasing their feeding frenzy, all the baby sharks leapt up from their prey and created an impenetrable wall around their father/mother. The bazooka blast rained baby blood and shark flesh down upon the deck, but the Clinton/Texas shark remained unharmed.

As the smoke began to clear, he/she just smiled, giving DMX a rudimentary thumbs-up with one of its pectoral fins as it kept on birthing babies.

The Clinton/Texas shark then turned its attention to T-Pain, who was hiding underneath a pile of Buzzfeed carcasses.

"HAVING ALL THESE BABIES MAKES ME HUNGRY FOR SOME DARK MEAT," he/she said, lunging in the rapper's direction.

His lasts words were a high-pitched scream he normally would've needed auto-tune to hit.

"Where my dogs at?!" DMX asked himself existentially.

The only survivors near the pool were a handful of young hipsters. One of them was sitting by the pool, rocking back and forth in a semi-catatonic state.

"The Arctic Monkeys... were more fun than Arcade Fire..." he mumbled to himself, "but... not so musically inclined. I would put them number 8... for indie rock bands young... adults listened to in 2006...."

"Run, motherfucker!" DMX screamed in his direction. "Those sharks gon' eat yo ass, nigga!"

But his warnings fell on deaf ears, and the kid just kept rambling about C-list indie bands until he was devoured.

Staring in disbelief, DMX lost all hope of trying to save the stupid white kids. Slinging his bazooka over his shoulder, he spun around and bolted back up the stairs to the wheelhouse.

"What's the word, y'all?" DMX asked the Admiral and Hillary. "Them sharks gon' be up in here quick!"

While the carnage unfolded by the pool, Admiral Rodgers had been listening to the radio and plotting a course to Trump Island. "Shit," he said, "I just learned that Israel is about to get hit by ISIS sand sharks. Somehow their defenses malfunctioned, looks to be a cyber attack...."

"Forget about Israel," Hillary said. "We've got to get Trump Island! Who knows when they'll fire those nukes?"

"Clint," DMX interjected, "we gotta stop these muthafuckin' sharks before we do anything else!"

The three of them looked down at the pool area, where the Clinton/Texas shark and its babies were finishing off the last scraps of the Buzzfeeders. There was a hunger in their eyes that would never be satisfied until they ate every last person onboard.

"We don't have much time," Rodgers said, "but I have an idea of how we might be able to stop this."

"How?" Clinton asked.

"I was able to dig up some intel from the NSASA."

"Who?"

"They're the National Security Agency that monitors the NSA."

"Jesus..." Hillary said, "I didn't even know they existed!"

"Thank God they do," the Admiral replied. "They got us files on Ray Kurzweil and his shark procedures on Trump Island. I learned how the Singularity transmission process works, and that Trump ordered experiments on Tibetan monks and even the porn star Alexis Texas."

"Which would explain why *my husband* is now a fucking shark..." Hillary huffed.

"Yes," Rodgers continued. "Kurzweil perfected his shark process on Trump Island. Through the creation of these cybernetically enhanced animal/humanoid hybrids, he was able to accomplish his perverse Singularity, but apparently the possibility of reproduction with a purely human host was never taken into account.... The unintended consequence seems to be the creation of a hive mind between parent and offspring, functioning something like a mainframe computer."

"What are you sayin', dawg?" DMX asked.

"What I am saying is that these sharks are all part of the same system, and the parent controls the others."

"I still don't understand a fuckin' thing you sayin'," DMX said. "What I wanna know is, how do we kill it?"

"You don't, because you can't," Hilary said in a solemn tone. "It doesn't even need its babies to protect it. This shark is so far outside of biological laws, when you have sex with it, you join it. That means it can morph its body to contain other entities and energies. A bomb won't stop that. That god damn bitch Alexis Texas, who screwed my husband through the last decade, she just had to do it one last time as a fucking shark. He had sex with that porn shark and melded with it in the process. When you have sex with these sharks, your consciousness is absorbed into their bodies. Therefore, if *I* could consummate with this shark, I could possibly direct its course...."

"Wait a sec, President," the Admiral said, "Are you saying you are going to engage in *intercourse* with a shark that is half porn star and half your husband?"

"Yes, because..."

"...if you join it, you'll be able to control its consciousness!"

"I can try," Clinton replied. "I was never able to do that very well while he was still human, but this isn't just about fidelity anymore, this is survival we're talking about."

"Do you know what this means, Madam President?"

"Yes, I do. I must fuck that shark to save the world."

"Damn, Clint," DMX said. "You go hard, girl!"

"I go where my country needs me to go, Mr. X."

The Admiral just shook his head and said, "You understand

that you would be *stuck* with your husband in the body of a shark and a porn star, most likely for the remainder of your existence."

"On the campaign trail, I said I would go to Hell and back for this country. Well, here's my chance to prove it!"

The Admiral manned the helm while Hillary marched down the stairs with DMX, who now had Epstein in tow. They'd caught him hiding in the trunk with all the life vests.

"Why do I have to be here?" Epstein whined, "I should be back up there, guiding the Admiral to the island!"

"Change of plans," Clinton said. "You don't deserve this, Epstein, but I'm giving you a chance to redeem your sorry ass—as bait. Do it, Mr. X."

"Wait!" the statutory rapist screamed. "NOOOOO!!!"

DMX nodded and threw him into the pool of sharks.

"SORRY BUDDY," the Clinton/Texas shark boomed from across the deck, "BUT YOU KNOW ABOUT YOUNG APPETITIES."

"DMX," Hillary said, looking on as the pervert was devoured by perversions of nature, "are you afraid to die?"

"Nah," he replied, grabbing an ax off the wall beside the fire extinguisher. "But even if I do, I'll go down helping the President, proving all the haters wrong. DMX ain't no joke; he still the realest nigga, goin' down as a straight shark killa."

"Mr. X, you're a great American," President Clinton said. "Just help me get to Bill, and I'll take the rest from there."

"What y'all really want!?" DMX barked as he charged forward, swinging his ax like a madman. "Stop / Drop / I'm shuttin' down these motherfuckin' sharks! / Oh / No / That's how Rough Ryders roll, nigga!"

Chopping off shark heads and fins left and right, DMX cleared a path for Hillary, holding off the voracious baby megalodons as they worked their way over to her husband.

"I KNOW THAT LOOK, HILL," the Clinton/Texas shark said. "YOU ARE PLOTTING SOMETHING. OH BOY, YOU HAVE THAT LOOK LIKE YOU'RE GONNA GIVE ME SEX IN EXCHANGE FOR SOMETHING. I'M SORRY HONEY, BUT I DON'T WANT TO SHARE THIS BODY WITH YOU. I'M FINALLY FREE OF YOU, AND NOW I GET TO BE WITH MY TRUE LOVE, ALEXIS TEXAS, FOREVER."

"Bill," Hillary began, "you have always been so selfish, ambivalent, and hurtful. Everyone in your life was just a piece of meat you had to taste. Being a shark fits you after all!"

"I LOVE BEING A SHARK, HONEY. I KNOW IT'S BEEN A WHILE SINCE WE'VE BEEN INTIMATE, BUT I'M GONNA EAT YOUR PUSSY AND THEN YOUR WHOLE BODY."

The Clinton/Texas shark lunged at her then, and it was in that moment Hillary realized she had failed. As a woman, as a wife, and as the President of the United States.

"NOOOOOO!!!!"

Tackling her out of the way at the very last second, Admiral Rodgers took the shark's pussy bite for her.

"Do it, Madam President!" the Admiral screamed as he was devoured from the waist down. "Do it for... America.... Please, Hill... ary.... Make... my sacrifice... MEAN something!"

Before he could say another word, the Clinton/Texas shark snapped up his upper half as well, swallowing it whole.

"UGGGHH, SO FULLLL..." the monster groaned, belching as it flopped over on its side.

Seeing its huge erection, Hillary knew what she had to do. For the first time in years, she wanted her husband's cock deep inside her.

Ripping off her clothes, she pulled aside her panties, took a running start, jumped and scissor-slid through all the gore, landing right on it.

"MY WIFE IS RAPING ME!!!" the shark screamed while ejaculating, "HELP ME, MY BABIES!!!"

The baby sharks gathered together, but Hillary was already morphing with her husband and Alexis. With no one to control their actions, they turned their collective attention to DMX instead.

"A'ight," he said, cocking back his ax. "Let's do dis."

He made a valiant effort against them, but there were far too many for him to kill the whole entire school. Dodging his final swing, one of the baby sharks tore into his guts.

The blood of DMX spilled onto the deck, and with his last heartbeat he witnessed something new being born.

Chapter 11

Avnat, Israel

Netanyahu stood with the Israeli troops, facing a Red Sea full of ISIS sharks. There was a fear in their eyes they'd never shown before in any previous battle. Religious Jews believed it was Yahweh who protected Israel, but it was always their advanced technology that kept them safe.

It was this technology that had been keeping Israel safe since it was first established in 1948. Without the aid of its sophisticated defenses and weaponry, Israel would have been wiped off the planet by its enemies long ago.

It wasn't China that had invented the ability to control magnetic properties, it was Israel, but like most electronic products, China had simply stolen it.

Inspired by the Marvel supervillain and Holocaust survivor, Magneto, they believed this power could protect their people from another genocide. Missiles fired by Hamas and Hezbollah from the neighboring territories were incapable of penetrating their magnetic force fields.

Normally Israel would have felt safe, but eight hours had passed since the virus infected their systems. Now that their force fields were down, along with their Internet and the rest of their computerized defenses, even the scientists who were secular Jews accepted that their survival really was in the hands of Yahweh.

The ISIS sand sharks surged forth, an army of man, beast, and machine— creatures whose sole purpose was the destruction Israel, clearing the way for the End of Times predicted in the Hadith.

Netanyahu had always believed this day would come.

Years before, he'd traveled to the United States to enlist their aid. At the time, he'd been convinced it was the Iranians who'd spell their doom, imploring the Americans to forbid Iran from obtaining nuclear materials.

But Iran never did strike Israel, and they too would have to face the Sunni sharks in battle.

Netanyahu watched the mass of fins as they swam onto shore, passing from water to sand unhindered. The Israeli soldiers stood with their guns at ready, but General Eizenkot withheld the order to open fire.

Intel had reported that these sharks were suicide bombers, each of them loaded with enough explosives to destroy everything in a fifty-mile radius. Shooting them here would be suicide for them as well.

Netanyahu turned his back to the incoming ISIS sharks, preparing to address his troops.

"My brothers and sisters of Israel," he began, "these could be the last words you will ever hear. We came to this land to find peace. To find safety from those who sought to exterminate us. The Final Solution, as the Nazis called it. All we ever wanted was a place we could call home. I will admit, I honestly don't know whether Yahweh exists or not, but the land He promised no longer does. We had to become wolves in order to survive, turning the Palestinians into sheep. And yet, now that the sharks are the wolves, I can see that God has failed all of his of children. Adam did not fail God, God failed Adam in his creation."

Netanyahu shed a tear as the sharks drew ever closer. Looking out upon the faces of his people, bereft of all hope, he looked up to the sky and said to God, "You let the Holocaust happen. You let these sharks, perversions of your laws, exist. If you are real, then you must save us. Save your chosen people!"

The ISIS sharks all laughed at Netanyahu, praying to a god that didn't exist.

"YOU DO NOT WORSHIP THE TRUE GOD," they

declared in unison. "THE ONLY TRUE PEOPLE OF THE BOOK ARE THOSE WHO FOLLOW THE ONLY TRUE BOOK, THE QURAN, AND FOLLOW ITS EVERY WORD. ALLAH IS READY TO PUNISH THE JEWS. WE WILL FEED ON THE FLESH OF THE REAL TERRORISTS. ALLAH HU AHKBAR!!!"

Netanyahu may have said goodbye to Israel, but he still needed to say goodbye to his family. As the sharks charged their ranks, he took out his phone.

Only the number wouldn't work. Pressing buttons, he found that the only thing he could access was a single new text message.

The contact had no photo, and its name was listed simply as "Anonymous".

"Your prayers are answered, Prime Minister," Anonymous had texted, "but in exchange, you must share your land with Palestine."

"What the hell...?" Netanyahu said, unable to believe it. "God... texts?"

His doubts were put to rest when Israel's force fields suddenly switched back on, stopping the advancing sharks in mid-swim.

Stuck in place, they could neither retreat into the water nor hide in the sand. Those that had already surfaced remained chomping and confused in mid-air, wondering what was preventing them from tearing into their prey.

"God has heard my prayers!" Netanyahu exclaimed. "We are saved!"

The assembled soldiers all gasped as laser beams shot out of the sharks' eyes, but they weren't aimed at them—they were aimed up at the sky instead. Connecting with the electromagnetic currents of the force field, together the beams created a giant, three-dimensional face.

Netanyahu looked up in awe as the face took shape in the sky above them. "It is the face of Yahweh!" he proclaimed.

"Wait, Prime Minster!" a solider called out. "It is not Yahweh, but the face of Guy Fawkes, you know? The mask from *V for Vendetta*!"

"I see…" Netanyahu said in a sober tone. "It is the Anonymous after all. There is no God, just as I thought.…"

"Correct, Prime Minister," the Guy Fawkes mask confirmed in its distorted voice.

"I don't care," Netanyahu replied. "I never counted on God, but I certainly didn't count on a non-Israeli hacker group coming to our rescue. But, you have saved us, so we thank you!"

"We have," Anonymous said, "and we will expect you to uphold your end of the bargain as well, sharing your land with the Palestinians. Right now, though, there is much more at stake. Unfortunately, we have only saved you temporarily.…"

The terrorist sharks remained immobile as their lasers projected the webcast hologram.

"What do you mean?" the Prime Minister asked. "What now? Are there to be even more sharks?"

"No," Anonymous replied. "Not yet at least. It is nukes, not sharks you must worry about now."

"Nukes?!" Netanyahu cried.

"Yes, we're afraid so. Donald Trump, Vladimir Putin, Yoweri Museveni, and Xi Jinping have all joined forces on a secret island, stockpiling nuclear weapons designed by Ray Kurzweil, the same man responsible for the ISIS Sharks of Singularity. These are no ordinary warheads; these are Nukes of Singularity. Once they are fired, they will be unstoppable. They possess enough consciousness to evade all defenses."

"No!" the Prime Minister cried. "Stop them, you must! Use your hacking skills!"

"We can't. Kurzweil has created a technology so advanced, even we cannot infiltrate it."

"Goddamn Kurzweil, I never trusted that bastard!"

"He was a good man, but Trump has turned him to the dark side," Anonymous replied, pausing before adding, "The God you once believed in probably does not exist, but He may be the only one who can help you now. If not, the Earth will become a land of suffering."

Chapter 12

Trump Island, Brunch Bungalow

Putin's *Hellraiser* hooks shredded their way through the jungle until they reached human flesh. Each of them dug into a different member of the *Shark Tank/Predator* alliance, slowly dragging them screaming into the bungalow.

Putin looked on in confusion as the men were piled up beside the table. "I didn't do that!" he gasped. "Those hooks were meant for you, Trump!"

"I know," Trump said, looking over at Kurzweil. "Now that you've captured the intruders, I want you to make these bozos into those things from *Hellraiser*. Putin, too. Make him look like Pinhead; that seems fitting. I want you to make me some Cenobites of Singularity."

"What?" Putin protested. "No, you can't!"

"Ray, shut this loser up, will you?"

Manipulating a strange device he held in hand, Kurzweil once again took control of Putin's hook chains. Sending them flying in all directions, he had each of them extract several nails from the deck boards, whipping them right at Putin's head.

"ARRRRRGGGHHHH!!!"

"Fear not, Putin," Kurzweil said, expertly controlling the placement of each nail. "The *Hellraiser* films were a major inspiration for my Singularity thesis. These chains are just machines, working to do your will. Well, *our* will, now!"

"NOOOOO!!! God damn you! It hurts!" Putin screamed, blood streaming down his face. "Just kill me, please! Don't make me like the sharks!"

"I'll make you into something much more," Trump said with pride. "You will bear witness to the end of the world as a member of my Trumpocalypse army."

While Kurzweil did his work, Trump looked down at the bloody pile of men who'd been dragged into the bungalow. Only Mark Cuban, Arnold Schwarzenegger, Carl Weathers, and Adrian Brody were still breathing.

"Do these guys next," Trump ordered Kurzweil. Then, looking over at his horrified assistant, he continued, "And you? You're fired, Omarosa. I'm bored with your ass. Ray—throw her together with Carl Weathers; they'd make a cute couple."

"Very well, sir," Kurzweil agreed.

Shooting one of Putin's hooks through Omarosa's neck, Kurzweil used his free ones to string up Weathers, Cuban,

Schwarzenegger, and Brody in similar fashion, holding them all on their feet. Then, walking up to each of them, he commenced inserting small metallic discs into their mouths, almost like he was giving them communion.

"This is the body of Singularity," Kurzweil told the dazed and bloodied group. "You will now be everlasting...."

Swallowing the chips on command, their tortured bodies began their transformations as Kurzweil manipulated his remote, programming their new Singularity forms to do his and his master's will. Spreading outward from the dissolving wafers in their stomachs, Singularity nanobots spread throughout their bodies and joined with their biological cells.

Their bodies contorted and shifted into a new species that was no longer recognizably human, but Cenobite, or Cenobyte as Kurzweil would call it. Together they stood before their new masters, deathly white skins contrasting with their black leather suits.

"Putin, Shark Tankers, Predators—you were never going to win or escape," Trump informed them with smug smile. "I just wanted some new toys to play with, before I blew up the world!"

"NOOO!!!" Putin bellowed, resisting Kurzweil's powers just long enough to fire off a hook in Trump's direction.

Hitting him in the crotch, it bounced off with a harmless *PING*.

"Ray," Trump laughed, "get this loser under control."

With the single press of a button, Putin felt the last vestiges of his former self disappear, subsumed by the machines that now controlled his fully Cenobyte form.

"I lied to you, Puthead," Trump said to the Pinhead-looking Putin. "You never were my special guest of honor. None of you were. I'm afraid your sacrifices were a necessary evil, clearing the way for myself and the Alpha Billionaire Buttrons to take over."

"Billionaire... Buttrons?" Larry David asked, crawling out from under the brunch table.

"Yes!" Trump proclaimed. "At first I thought the term was ridiculous myself, but then I remembered I am Donald Trump, and if I could make this hair of mine look awesome, I could make the term Buttron just as amazing. Donald Trump can make anything great! Where my anus used to be is now a nuclear reactor, charging my invincible body. It gives me eternal life and makes me indestructible! In this new age, the term Buttron will become synonymous with God."

"Can I be one too?" David asked, sheepishly.

"No! You are loser, Larry David, but you can still behold our glory...."

"Eh," David said, shrugging his shoulders. "Better to be rejected as a Buttron than accepted as a Cenobyte."

"Fellow Buttrons," Trump called out. "Come to me, now! It is time! Come to your leader!"

From the other side of the island, they heard the sound of rockets igniting, and seconds later a group of humanoid figures with metallic lower halves were touching down on the beach outside the bungalow.

Two of them looked familiar to David; he remembered seeing them in many the political ad. The Koch brothers. There were several other billionaires among their ranks as well, and while

David couldn't quite place them, he knew that he was standing in the presence of some of the most powerful and ruthless men in the world.

Trump then reached down and ripped his pants off, exposing his own lower half. Along with the rest of his body from the waist down, his cybernetic cock and balls had been forged from pure steel.

As Trump turned to address his assembled Buttrons, David noticed the white hot glow emanating from his rectal area, the nuclear power source granting him eternal life. Through the skin of Trump's back, he could literally see his powerful metallic heart beating, pumping blood to the rest of his cybernetic organs. It was all powered from his nuclear anus, giving Trump eternal life and invincibility.

"Uh, well I'll be," David said, "you really are a Buttron after all!"

Kurzweil stood with reverence before the sight of his creations. He may have been a prisoner on Trump Island, but right about now he felt like a god amongst gods.

And yet, like the monkeys who gave birth to man, he was still a slave to the laws of natural selection. He understood this biological process well, and those who were not Buttrons would either be enslaved or go extinct.

As a result, Kurzweil had made Trump promise that once the Nukes of Singularity were unleashed upon the world, he would be allowed to become a Billionaire Buttron as well. Maybe not an Alpha, but a Buttron just the same.

"Wake up, Ray," Trump barked at Kurzweil. "There will be plenty of time for reflection *after* the bombs drop. The world needs to hear me speak; go get it set up. It's time for the people to meet their new leader."

"Very well," Kurzweil said, punching buttons on his remote. A whole array of cameras descended from the bungalow's ceiling and rose up from its floor, ready to broadcast Trump and his fellow Billionaire Buttrons to every major network on the planet.

While he prepared to speak, Trump instructed Kurzweil to go and wake up the Nukes. "They need to be ready for their mission," he said. "These ISIS losers will soon realize the purpose of their existence."

The ISIS members who became Nukes had been hand-selected by Caliph Bakr himself for their most critical mission yet—the final nail in the coffin of the Jahiliyyah. Kurzweil transformed them into part man, part nuclear missile, 100% suicide bomber. Staring out through the tips of their multi-megaton warheads, their human identities were still fully apparent in their brown, hate-filled eyes.

Although they'd grown impatient waiting, they took solace in the knowledge that soon they'd be joining their 72 virgins in Paradise.

Their day had finally arrived.

"My fellow Billionaire Buttrons," Trump directed them, "get ready for the camera, but don't block out the ISIS Nukes. The world needs to see their faces."

He nodded to Kurzweil and said, "It's go time."

Kurzweil activated the cameras as commanded, introducing the world to the *real* Donald Trump and his fellow Buttrons for the first time. Behind them was a sizable stockpile of living, sentient nuclear weapons.

Trump gave a prideful nod to the camera. "Are you with your family?" he asked. "Good, because at least you can die with them. None of you are worthy of life. Humanity as a whole is nothing but a bunch of losers. The sharks, the attacks, it was all me, and the leaders of your most powerful nations are now all dead. Anarchy will spread across the world, but if you are among the lucky ones to survive my Singularity nukes, then you will fall under my leadership."

He paused here to let the news sink in.

"Look at us. Behold. We cannot die; we are the gods who will restore this Earth in our image. Those who are smart and want to survive will worship us as gods, but we are not heartless gods. You now have exactly 30 seconds to say goodbye to your loved ones before we unleash the ISIS Nukes of Singularity." "NOT IF WE CAN HELP IT!!!"

ACT 5

Final Chapter

The Battle of Trump Island

The cameras panned out to the oceanfront, where thousands upon thousands of sharks were presently surfing toward Trump Island.

Leading them was a megalodon-sized Billary Shark of Singularity.

All of the sharks were controlled by His/Her thoughts, including those birthed earlier by Clinton/Texas and others they'd rounded up along the way. It was like a tsunami of teeth and fins heading straight for Trump Island.

"Puthead," Trump said, "gather your Cenobytes, and teach these sharks the true meaning of pain!"

The Buttrons and Nukes looked on as the Cenobytes

marched out onto the beach as ordered.

As the shark wave crashed before them, the Tibetan mural was instantly erased from the sand at their feet, and the battle for Trump Island had officially begun.

Pinhead Putin fired his chain hooks at the incoming sharks, peeling off their skins and slicing them in half with ease. Several of them he plucked up from the surf, using their bodies to bludgeon their brethren to death.

The others tried their best to help him, but there were just too many sharks for them to deal with. It was the sharks that did the torturing, not the Cenobytes, ripping them all to pieces bite by bite. One by one, the mighty Cenobytes were overwhelmed by the invading sharks, littering the beach with their pale white, leather-clad corpses.

"NOOOO!!!" Kurzweil screamed. "My Cenobytes! I'm not a Buttron yet, and I don't want to die!"

"YOU WILL DIE, KURZWEIL!!!" the Billary shark boomed, "OR I WILL MAKE YOU MY SLAVE!!!"

"Stop her!" Trump screamed. "Stop her now, Ray!"

"This is... an unintended consequence of Singularity..." Kurzweil stammered, slowly backing away. "Mating was not supposed to happen! That shark with Bill and Hillary Clinton and... well, God knows what else... it could absorb every last one of us! She could probably even absorb the Nukes!"

"Nonsense," Trump said as Kurzweil tried to run away. He stuck a finger up his metallic anal cavity and Kurzweil flew into his grip.

The sharks were almost upon them now.

"Buttrons, attack!" Trump ordered them, dragging Kurzweil back into the bungalow. "I shall unleash the nukes!"

The Buttrons activated their leg rockets and blasted off through wave after wave of sharks, swinging whirlwind fists to pulverize them. The tide ran red with shark blood and guts, but soon it became apparent that even the mighty Buttrons would not be enough to stop them.

Watching the battle unfold from the veranda, Trump knew that his time was short. He felt fear for the first time in his existence as a Buttron.

"You have failed me," he said, turning to face Kurzweil.

"What?!" the scientist cried in horror as Trump advanced upon him. "But... but... but... you said you would let me be a Buttron! I christened that word, even."

"To be a Buttron is to be a winner," Trump said, taking Kurzweil by his lab coat, "and you, you are a loser. I no longer have any use for you."

Lifting Kurzweil overhead and effortlessly tossing him out a hundred yards, Trump watched Billary catch his flailing body right in her savagely gnashing jaws.

The only two Buttrons left, the Koch brothers refocused their offensive on Billary, hoping to turn the tide of their losing battle by taking out the sharks' leader.

"KOCH BROS, ATTACK!!!" the Koch brother Buttrons boomed in unison.

Positioning himself behind Charles, David Koch jammed his giant metal penis up his brother's nuclear anal cavity, using them to magnify their combined powers.

"INITIATING KOCH SUPER STRIKE."

The Koch brother Buttrons blasted forth together as Billary leapt high into the air, narrowly dodging their power attack.

As Billary descended upon them, the Koch brothers held each other tight, screaming as they were swallowed in one savage bite. Instantly they dissolved inside her stomach, spending their finals moments being turned into shark shit.

"Enough!" cried Trump.

Disgusted by the loss of his fellow Buttrons, he went over to the Nukes and glanced back at Billary. "They were losers, just like you," he said. "You, your husband, and that skank whore inside you. You won't be able to stop me!"

Trump pressed the launch button and stood back with folded arms, smiling smugly as the rockets ignited.

"ALLAH HU AKABAR!!!" the Nukes all cried together, reveling in religious ecstasy as their countdown sequence began.

"TEN... NINE... EIGHT... SEVEN... SIX..."

"NOOOOOOOOOO!!!!" Billary screamed, lunging toward them.

"FIVE... FOUR... THREE... TWO... ONE...."

The ISIS Nukes of Singularity achieved lift-off, each of them programmed to hit every nation on Earth, but all they hit was the back of Billary's throat as she fell upon them, shooting her up into the sky.

Falling back down to the Earth with a deafening thud, a huge black cloud of smoke exploded from her gaping shark mouth.

Billary had successfully absorbed the ISIS Nukes of Singularity

The bungalow had been reduced to cinders, but Trump was still alive. He now looked something like a Terminator robot with its skin burnt off, but he hadn't given up yet.

Meanwhile, the cameras continued to roll.

"Losers!" Trump cried. "Don't you see? I WILL NEVER DIE!!!"

Billary felt the eyes of the world watching. She was connected to all of them through the machines. She felt their pain and their fear, but also their joy. The Singularity inside of her was giving her more power, fueled by the Nukes and the Buttrons. In that moment she felt omnipotent, like she could do anything with the force of her thoughts alone.

Focusing her mind on the Pinhead Putin corpse, she manipulated the chains still connected to its back. As they floated toward her, she thought of her favorite book, *Moby Dick*, and how Trump was an Ahab that would sink the world.

Before he could dodge or escape, she'd wound them tight around his body. Wrapping them over his screaming mouth, Billary muzzled Trump into silence as he coughed and choked upon the cold, bitter metal. Imprisoned and bound, he found himself powerless, chained to Billary's mighty body. Her Singularity was stronger than his, and just like Ahab, he would live out his remaining days trapped in a net of his own creation.

Billary looked into the cameras and felt all of human consciousness inside her. She was struck by the paradox of how insignificant she really was and how much power she now held.

The wisdom of her human soul combined with her powers of Singularity, and she could see how the world was plunging into total chaos. Nations were falling, and new powers were going to rise. This new technology had so much potential to help humankind, but it would require great guidance to be a force of good and not evil.

With great clarity in her shark heart, Billary prepared to address the world.

"This terrorist bound to me is a symbol of the fate that awaits us all in this new and dangerous world. A world where human beings are no longer strong enough to protect themselves against technology driven mad by mad men. To save us, I knew I had to become like the sharks that led this global attack, but now the sharks are under my control. I know most of you don't love or even like me, but I have sacrificed my life in order to protect yours. This man, who will be forever strapped to my body, is just one of the many monsters this new age will spawn. I shall be the one who stands in their way.

I vow to spend my life patrolling land and sea, stopping any man, woman, or shark from harming the innocent, bringing justice to every shore.

Thank you and God bless. I gladly serve as your world's watcher and humble servant, Hillary and Bill Clinton."

Larry David walked in front of the camera then, slow clapping and nodding with approval of Billary. He gave a thumbs up to the cameras and then a middle finger to Trump, who could only moan in agony, rattling the chains that bound him.

David waved to the cameras and said, "You really gotta try the omelets here, delicious!"

Billary remained somber and silent in that moment, but she

could hear the cheering and applause coming to her from all around the globe. As the euphoria rose inside her, she wondered if this was how it felt to be God.

About the Authors

Arthur Graham is a professional editor, writer, and book critic currently residing in Salt Lake City, Utah. He is an accomplished noveler, storyist, and publishite by all accounts. His work has been unfairly compared to that of Charles Bukowski, William S. Burroughs, Hunter S. Thompson, and Kurt Vonnegut, Jr. Once a promising purveyor of fine literary fiction, he has since been reduced to writing about sharks instead. For more of his books and reviews, find him online at Goodreads.com.

About the Authors

Christoph Paul is a musician, podcaster, and YA & Bizarro Fiction author of *The Passion of the Christoph* and *Slasher Camp for Nerd Dorks*, published by Eraserhead Press. He is the co-publisher and editor of New English Press. He plays in rock band Moses Moses & was guitar player/singer of The Only Prescription, but still wishes he was a gangsta rapper. He has even told people he is Drake's full-Jewish brother Rake.

For fun he likes to read YA and Bizarro, get angry in a bar while watching the Miami Dolphins lose, live Tweeting The Bachelor while watching it with his girlfriend, and gardening with his cats. For fun and money he writes Bizarro Erotica under the pen name Mandy De Sandra, who was covered in VICE, Huffington Post, Jezebel, and AV Club.

Sometimes, he dresses up like a famous serial killer and interviews literary types on YouTube.

He is repped by Veronica Park at the Corvisiero Literary Agency.

WALK HAND IN HAND INTO EXTINCTION
Edied by Christoph Paul and Leza Cantoral

SOCIAL MEDIA FOR ANTI-SOCIALS
by Christoph Paul

SLASHER CAMP FOR NERD DORKS
by Christoph Paul

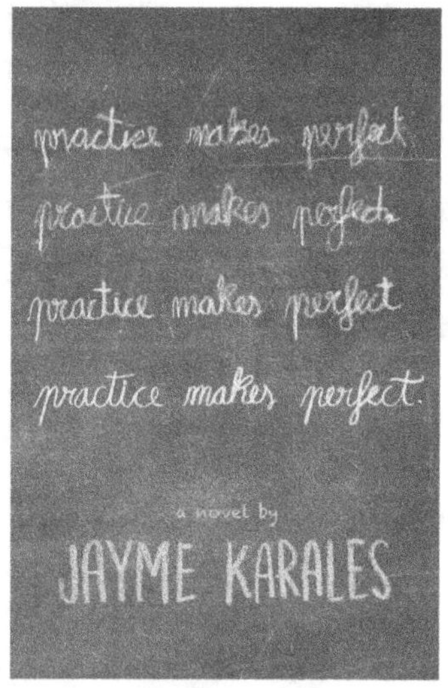

PRACTICE MAKES PERFECT
by Jayme Karales